UNDERCOVER GIRL

#2...Fugitive

by Christine Harris

scholastic inc.

New York   Toronto   London   Auckland   Sydney
Mexico City   New Delhi   Hong Kong   Buenos Aires

For Marla, who knows what it's like

No part of this publication may be reproduced, stored in a retrieval system, or transmitted in any form or by any means, electronic, mechanical, photocopying, recording, or otherwise, without written permission of the publisher. For information regarding permission, write to Permissions Department, Scholastic Australia, PO Box 579, Lindfield, New South Wales, Australia 2070.

ISBN 0-439-76126-3

All rights reserved. Published by Scholastic Inc., 557 Broadway, New York, NY 10012, by arrangement with Omnibus Books, an imprint of Scholastic Australia.

SCHOLASTIC, APPLE PAPERBACKS, and associated logos are trademarks and/or registered trademarks of Scholastic Inc.

12 11 10 9 8 7 6 5 4 3 2 1   5 6 7 8 9 10/0

Printed in the U.S.A.

First American edition, November 2005

1.

Jesse ran. The narrow path twisted around trees and boulders. Her sneakers snapped twigs and scattered fallen leaves. Low-hanging branches slapped her face and ripped at her hair.

Behind her a dog barked, setting off the whole pack. She pictured them straining at their leashes, mouths curled back from sharp teeth, drooling. She checked her watch. Ten of her fifteen-minutes' head start had gone.

Once she had longed to run outdoors with the wind in her face. But not like this. Not trying to keep ahead of dogs that were trained to hunt. *They go for the throat first.*

Unconsciously, Jesse flung one hand up to touch the soft skin of her neck.

She couldn't escape by leaving the path and going cross-country. Out there were high electric fences topped with barbed wire. *What if I climb a tree?* she thought. *No, they'd still find me. And I'd have to come down sometime. The dogs would just wait.* The only way to survive was to keep moving forward.

Mouth dry, heart pounding, she burst into a clearing. There was a lake in front of her, straddled by an arched bridge. *Over the bridge or through the water?*

Jesse blinked and craned her head forward. The bridge rails seemed to be squirming. A short dash brought her close enough to be sure. The hairs on her arms stood up as she realized what she was looking at.

2.

Snakes curled around the rails.

Jesse's stomach tightened.

She turned toward the deeper part of the water. She could swim, and the dogs would lose her scent, but she hesitated. Escape that way was too obvious. C2 was an organization that dealt in secrets. Nothing was ever straightforward. If swimming across the lake appeared easy, then it probably wasn't.

Barking echoed through the trees behind her. The dogs were catching up. If she failed, they would turn her into mincemeat.

She headed for the bridge. *Don't think about what's hanging off the rails.*

"Go!" The rough sound of her own shout

spurred her on. Perspiration, strangely cold, trickled down the back of her neck. She kept her eyes focused straight ahead, her elbows close to her body.

A snake thrust its head toward her as she approached. She swerved, half-expecting to feel fangs pierce her arm. Heat surged through her body. But she passed untouched.

At last, clear of the bridge, feet on solid ground, Jesse checked behind her.

The dog pack erupted from the bushes on the other side of the water. *How could they have caught up so fast?* She shot along the path as it veered left and widened into a track. A familiar black minivan with tinted windows was parked there.

Suddenly, the van's sliding door opened. Jesse leaped inside. The door shut. Her chest heaved as she gasped for air. Liam, her C2 partner, sat in the back. His pale, pock-marked face looked like the moon, with all craters visible.

Before either of them could speak, the van was surrounded by barking dogs. Jesse flinched as the dogs threw themselves against the doors, their nails scratching the paint.

The driver shouted, "Call off those mutts."

Outside, a sharp whistle, then a shout from the dog handler subdued the pack.

Finally, it was quiet, except for Jesse's labored breathing.

"Congratulations, thumb sucker," said Liam. "Looks like you passed."

Jesse glared. *Does he have to call me that?*

As usual, Liam's hair pointed up like dry grass. But Jesse knew she couldn't look much better. Her left cheek stung. She touched it, then inspected her fingertips. There was a smear of blood on her index finger.

The driver turned the key and started the motor.

"Here." Liam handed Jesse the blindfold she had worn on their journey out to the training area.

Weird. They'll let me go through all this, but they won't tell me where I am.

As she slipped on the blindfold, it stuck to the perspiration on her forehead. "Were those snakes poisonous?"

"No."

She pushed her hands against her legs to stop them from trembling. "What was in the water?"

"You don't want to know," said Liam.

"Yes, I do." The van bounced over a rut, jarring Jesse's spine.

"Piranhas."

"P . . . p . . . real ones?"

Liam snorted.

Jesse wished she could see his face. "But I could've been killed!"

"You have to be tough to survive in this business."

"I don't think many bad guys stop in the middle of a chase to throw flesh-eating fish into puddles."

"No, but you need to make quick decisions under pressure. Often there's no simple answer. If you make the wrong choice, you die."

"What if I'd tried to swim?"

"I'd miss you," he said.

"Yeah right."

"But as I've said before, I could be lying."

"About missing me or the piranhas?"

Liam didn't answer.

3.

In C2's underground briefing room, Jesse sat beside Liam. She didn't look at him or speak. Why be polite to someone who almost let her die?

Maybe Director Granger had something over Liam, *forced* him to obey orders. *Like me,* she thought. C2 had raised her, Rohan, and Jai. Rohan had disappeared, and that left Jai as the only person she could fully trust. Providenza, the Director's office manager, was kind to her, but they had few chances to get to know each other better. Jesse had no real family, and she couldn't leave the C2 building on her own because the doors opened only to authorized palm-print identification.

Director Granger seemed to slide into the room rather than walk. His gray suit fit him well. His tie hung straight over a crisp blue shirt. Jesse wondered how long he spent checking his appearance in the mirror. *If he ever gets a speck of dirt on him, they should set off fireworks.* But no matter how dapper Granger looked or how polite his tone, something dark and dangerous lurked in his eyes.

"Good morning, Jesse . . . Liam."

Liam grunted.

Director Granger glanced at Jesse's scratched face. "Glad to hear your training session was successful."

Jesse said nothing.

"You're precious to us, my dear. After all, we here at C2 are your family."

Liam made a noise deep in his throat and put one hand over his mouth as though he had coughed. "Excuse me."

Director Granger shot him a look as he placed two folders on the table. "Your new assignment. Eyes only — read the material, memorize it, then leave the folder here."

Liam nodded.

Granger picked up a remote control from the table top and aimed it at a painting of purple flowers. The painting disintegrated, dot by dot, and was replaced by a computer screen.

A click of the remote brought up photographs of two men.

"This is Ari and Josef. Yesterday they entered this country illegally. Following a tip-off, C2 agents stopped and impounded the boat that brought them here. Unfortunately, the only man left on board was the skipper. Ari and Josef had already slipped ashore." Granger's face darkened.

Someone's in big trouble, thought Jesse. She wouldn't like to be the agents who arrived too late.

"Interrogation of the skipper did not reveal much. Thanks to some clumsy fool, there is no chance of extracting more. You'll have to work with what's there."

Jesse shivered. *No chance of more information? What did they do to that man?*

"I want you to find Ari." He zoomed in on one of the photographs. "Bring him to C2. You have three days to do it. We have information that Ari and Josef plan to leave the country again on Friday evening. We have another team searching tonight. You can begin fresh in the morning."

Granger stared at Jesse. "Get a good night's sleep. We've had enough blunders already in this matter."

She stared back calmly, but her mind was busy. *Why is he eyeballing me? Does he think I'm going to make a mistake?*

"Jesse, you're a child. People won't suspect you of being a secret agent. Perhaps they will tell you more. You completed your first assignment satisfactorily. I hope you will be successful again." Granger shifted his gaze to include Liam. "That applies to both of you. This assignment is important. We must have Ari."

Jesse peered at the face on the screen. Ari had dark skin, a longish nose, and full lips. His eyes seemed to be asking a question. There was a small scar on the outside corner of his left eye, and the lid drooped a little. In spite of that, it was a handsome face.

Granger leaned forward. "Do whatever it takes. I want that man brought in."

"What about the second man, Josef?" asked Liam.

Granger shrugged. "Josef is not important to us. We simply want Ari, as soon as possible." He straightened his tie, although it didn't need it. "But Josef will make it difficult to bring in his companion. He won't let you take him without a fight. He's clever, organized, ruthless — and he's a professional killer."

4.

Ten floors above street level, Jesse stood at the window in her room, adjusting her telescope. Street lights winked and vehicle headlights flashed. She focused on a young woman with a fondness for body piercing. So many rings lined her nostrils and eyebrows, she was a walking jewelry store. *I wonder if she leaks in the shower, with all those holes?*

"Bite me." She stepped back from the telescope. "Look at her."

"Bite me?" Jai raised his eyebrows.

She shrugged. "It's an expression I heard when I was outside."

"And those people are supposed to be normal?"

"What's *normal?*" said Jesse. "Horses can't vomit. Pigs can't put their heads back to look at the sky. You and I are geniuses. That's normal. For *us.*"

He put his eye to the telescope.

Jesse noticed that his hair was growing back. Michael and Roger, the C2 scientists, said they sometimes needed smooth skin for attaching electrodes that monitored brain waves. Now that Jesse was working on outside assignments, they had stopped shaving her head. Maybe they wanted her to look more normal. But Jai still had regular sessions in the laboratory. Jesse felt guilty, as though it were somehow her fault. Even though she knew it wasn't. She pushed her memories of the laboratory aside, refusing to dwell on them.

She stared out across the city. That man, Ari, was down there somewhere. He might be sipping coffee or making plans with his friend. Or was he checking nervously over his shoulder? Maybe he had walked past the young woman with all the body piercings. But now, he wasn't a fugitive. He was a target. *And I'm one of his hunters.*

"Do you wish you could hear what people on the street are saying?" asked Jai.

"No. I'd rather make it up."

Jai's voice was softer, more wistful than usual. *Is something bothering him?* wondered Jesse. He often wore his worries around for a while before he shared them with her.

There was a loud knock at the door.

Abruptly, Jai pulled back the telescope.

The door burst open.

Mary Holt, their carer, marched into the room. Head forward, frizzy hair framing her long face, she constantly reminded Jesse of a striking cobra. The suddenness of her entrances suggested attack.

Jesse looked sideways at Jai. His brown skin had faded to gray. A nerve twitched under his left eye. She was tempted to put her arm around his shoulders. But suggesting he had a weakness might draw unwelcome attention. She kept her arms hanging loosely at her sides.

Mary looked smug. "You two thought you were escaping, didn't you?"

5.

Jesse tensed. Then she noticed the small tray in Mary's hands.

"Extra vitamins and minerals are not required by a healthy person eating a balanced diet," said Jai. "And we have had our vitamin injection only recently."

"Healthy body, healthy mind." Mary put the tray on the round table and began counting out tablets from white containers.

She brought them first to Jai, with a glass of water. It would be spring water, poured from a suitably sealed bottle. Jesse amused herself by exaggerating the image of Mary in a full body suit with face mask and oxygen tank, pouring water into a glass.

The calcium tablet was dry but not too bad. The kelp smelled like rotten seaweed. But the cod liver oil ball made Jesse's stomach recoil. It was covered in a clear skin, like plastic. If it broke as she swallowed, cod liver oil burst out into her throat. It made her gag, and the taste lingered afterward.

Mary placed her hands on Jesse's upper arms and turned her toward the overhead light. "Tsk. Tsk. Look at the scratch on that face." Her fingertips were hot, as though she had just held a saucepan with both hands. She was so close, Jesse could clearly see the strange speck of brown in her right eye. Against the green iris, it was eerily like an extra pupil. Jesse wanted to pull free, but she forced herself to remain still.

Mary fetched antiseptic cream from the bathroom cabinet and dabbed it on Jesse's scratch. It stung a little, but Jesse didn't complain. Mary didn't ask how she was wounded. Did she already know?

Then, as Mary finally headed for the door, Jesse said, "Can I have my tongue pierced?"

Mary halted. "Can you *what*?" An ugly flush reddened her face.

"How about my belly button, then?"

"It's mutilation!"

"No, it's jewelry."

Mary resumed her path to the door. "Absolutely *not*." For the first time that Jesse could remember, Mary shut the door behind her. Although *shut* was an understatement. *Slammed* was more like it.

Jesse grinned at Jai. "She's coming around, I can tell. Actually, I want my ears pierced. But if you want a dog, start out by asking for a horse."

"We are surrounded, are we not?" he said.

So much for trying to cheer him up. But Jai was right. There were listening devices, movement sensors, laboratory doctors, and technology experts who tried — and failed — to hack into their computers.

Now Jesse did put one arm over Jai's thin shoulders and whispered, "One day, we'll get out of here."

He bowed his head.

"What else is bothering you? Tell me."

"I have been thinking about those other children in Operation IQ that your friend . . ."

"Liam is *not* my friend."

"He said one of them went insane."

She remembered Liam's sneer when he told her about the C2 boy who'd had a nervous breakdown and spent his days unable to do anything but build models from lollipop sticks.

Jai's high cheekbones cast faint shadows on his cheeks. "If that is true, and Rohan was sent away because he was sick, then maybe we will all break down. What if we are flawed?"

The sound of Rohan's name gave Jesse a jolt. Bold, funny, and brilliant with computers, he'd been like a brother to her and Jai. As far back as Jesse could remember, the three of them had been together. Until now. She did not believe the Director's claim that Rohan was sick and needed to be alone.

"Every human is flawed. No one is perfect," she said. "And we can't be sure there really are other IQ kids like us. Liam doesn't always tell the truth."

"Even child prodigies on the outside are sometimes mentally unstable."

"So? Sometimes they're not."

"A boy who played classical guitar sawed

off his own finger so that he would not have to practice."

There are some things I don't need to know. Jesse smiled for Jai. "You're the sanest person I know."

"How many people do you know?"

"Not many. But you're my favorite."

He glanced at the scratch on her face. "You are going outside again?"

Jesse nodded. She couldn't tell anyone about her assignment. The Director had stressed that. Besides, the more Jai knew, the more danger he could be in if things went wrong. And Jai was fragile. He worried about everything.

"Rohan has gone," he said. "Now it is just the two of us. If you do not return, I will be alone."

Jesse fixed her eyes on his. "I will *never* leave you alone, Jai. I promise."

Her smile hid doubts. The next day, she would begin hunting a man for C2. What would they do to him? And this man's companion was a killer. She hoped that she hadn't made a promise to Jai that she could not keep.

6.

Inside Liam's car, take-out food cartons and scrunched paper bags littered the floor. Jesse brushed crumbs off the seat before she climbed in. Instinctively, she wrinkled her nose. Somewhere among this mess was an unfinished hamburger — with pickles. She loved burgers, even though Mary would go crazy if she caught Jesse even sniffing one. But they were not so appetizing when they were days old.

"Been too busy saving the world to clean up." Liam folded his long legs into the car.

"People who save the world don't drive heaps like this." Jesse clicked her seat belt.

Liam picked up a crushed Chinese food

container from under his feet and hurled it over his shoulder. "No one spots this car when I'm following them. They're busy looking for some fancy model with tinted windows."

He had a point, but she refused to admit it aloud. "So this car is in disguise, then?"

"There's more to Betsy than meets the eye." He patted the dashboard.

Betsy? What kind of secret agent calls his car Betsy?

Liam pointed to the cigarette lighter. "Check that out. I just installed it."

She took out the lighter. Behind it was a flashing red light.

Liam frowned. He took a pen-sized scanner from his jacket pocket. Carefully, he ran it over the dashboard and around the car. When he pointed it at the floor beneath his feet, it too began to flash.

Making little sound, he slid out of the car, bent, and aimed the scanner. Then he thrust out his arm and plucked something loose. Checking left and right, he threaded his way around parked cars till he found a sleek red one.

Seconds later, he was back. The car rocked

as he slammed the door. Several papers floated into new positions. "It was a tracking device. That'll confuse them."

"Whose car did you put it on?" asked Jesse.

"The Director's." Liam smirked. "It'll be a bit of . . . uh . . . professional training for him. If he's lazy and doesn't check, whoever planted the tracker will follow the wrong car. That'll give us a head start."

"But won't that put him in danger?"

Liam shrugged. "He's a big boy. Besides, I've seen enough of those things to be pretty sure it's one of our gadgets."

"Any idea who put it there?" asked Jesse.

"It's not my friend, Hans, the practical joker. He's on assignment overseas. Besides, he wouldn't waste good surveillance equipment on me. It may have nothing to do with our current assignment. Or C2 could be keeping a close eye on us. They might let us do the hard work finding Ari, but plan to grab him before we can."

"They don't trust us," said Jesse.

"They don't trust *anyone*. And neither should you."

7.

"Here." Liam handed Jesse a small plastic card. "This transaction card gives you access to your bank account."

"I don't have a bank account." C2 provided what they thought she needed. And occasionally, Providenza sneaked her treats — chocolate most often, but sometimes videos, books, or clothes.

"You do now. Regular deposits will be made into a special account. There'll be times when you're working alone that you'll need money. You can't run to me every five minutes asking for things."

"I haven't asked for *any*thing," she said sharply.

"Not yet. Now you won't need to." He turned the ignition key.

An allowance. Awesome. Maybe the piranhas and wild dogs test was worth something after all. Jesse kept her expression neutral. It was safer to keep her emotions to herself. And Liam sounded grudging, as though she'd caused him a heap of trouble. And she *hadn't*.

Liam accelerated, making the tires screech. "Got your communicator?"

Jesse nodded. It was an ordinary watch till she pressed a button. Then she could send or receive messages. And she could choose either a voice or a text message.

"Try not to break this one." He drove out of the parking garage and turned right.

As always, she tried to look at everything around her all at once. It was so colorful and alive out here. Not like the sterile C2 building.

"What can you tell me about our target?" asked Liam.

"Ari is a janitor in a laboratory. He's been friends with the other man, Josef, for ten years. Yesterday, they entered the country illegally. Ari likes books, long-distance running, and Indian food. Educated in England, so his English is excellent. Married with three children. A flyer from an organization called Peace First was found on the boat."

"I have some contacts who hear things going down on the streets. I'll check with them to see what they know. You find out what you can from Peace First."

"Why does the Director want us to find a janitor who likes books?"

Liam threw her a look that she couldn't fathom. "We don't need to know why. We just need to know how. How to get him."

"What if he doesn't want to come?"

"You want to tell Granger that?"

"No." She remembered Director Granger's expression as he briefed them on their assignment. There must be more to this. Unless Ari's identity was a cover. Could he also be a killer?

"How do we know Ari's in this city?" she asked Liam. "He could have gone in any direction."

"Aha. Genius at work." There was a hint of sarcasm in Liam's voice. "Granger gave me an update this morning. Yesterday, a police officer saw two men who fit their descriptions acting suspiciously on an outer suburban road, and walking toward the city. The officer called headquarters, then got out to investigate. An hour later, the car was found abandoned. The police officer had vanished."

Hot prickles swept the back of Jesse's neck. Instinct told her that no one would see that policeman again. At least not alive.

8.

Jesse pushed open the door to the Peace First office and smiled brightly. "Hello."

The man she addressed barely looked up from his bundle of papers.

Notice where everybody is the moment you enter a room, Liam had told her. *You may have to run — or fight.* The Peace First office was large and untidy. As well as the man at the front desk, there was a middle-aged woman, a purple scarf around her neck, talking on the phone. At the back, two men focused intently on a computer screen. A young woman with red hair rattled the photocopier, as though she were annoyed with it. A plump, gray-haired woman folded papers. Six people in all.

"I want to volunteer." Jesse dropped her backpack.

The man looked up at her then. For someone who was all about peace, his own face looked as though it had been in a war. One eye was a little higher than the other, and there was a long scar on his right cheek. A burn, maybe? He was in his thirties, she guessed.

"You're a *kid*."

She knew that he saw a girl of medium height, with brown hair, thick bangs over brown eyes, and a smattering of freckles. Not someone to suspect.

"Yeah, I noticed that," she said with a toss of her head. "Kids want peace, too. Who suffers most in wars? Is it adults? No, it's *kids*!"

He softened his voice. "We appreciate the thought, but we'll be in trouble if you skip school to be here. Run along before someone notices you're gone."

"I'm home-schooled and I'm ahead in all subjects. I can easily take a day off. Give me a subject and I'll tell you what I know." She chanted in a sing-song voice, "The average person sheds one pound of skin per year. There are 336 dimples on a golf ball . . ."

The man held up one hand. "I get the picture."

The young woman at the photocopier turned to look at them. Her hair was so red that Jesse was tempted to grab a fire extinguisher. "I need help with these flyers, Brian," said the young woman.

Jesse placed a scrap of paper on the desk. "My dad gave me permission to be here. He says volunteer work is part of my education. Here's his cell-phone number, if you want to check."

"I give up." Brian shrugged. "But if there's trouble, you're on your own."

Jesse nodded. *So what's new?*

The young woman with the red hair beckoned her over. "My name's Harmony."

"I'm April," said Jesse.

"That's funny. It *is* April. What a coincidence."

Jesse laughed along with Harmony. *Next time I'll pick something less obvious.*

Harmony wore a brown T-shirt embossed

with the words MAKE CHOCOLATE NOT WAR. Heavy eyeliner made her eyes look huge. Jesse tried not to stare. *And either that's black lipstick or there's something seriously wrong with her liver.*

"Leave your backpack in that closet if you like."

As Jesse opened the closet door, she saw a small metal trash can to one side. It was stacked with take-out food containers. A spicy aroma still hung around the mangled packaging. *Ari likes Indian food.* But the Golden Turban was only two doors up the street, and Indian food was popular with lots of people.

Jesse's mind spun with questions. *Why had the Peace First flyer been on the boat?* She had to find the connection quickly. There wasn't much time. Josef killed people. *So why would he and Ari be interested in a peace group?*

9.

Harmony's desk was covered with bundles of flyers. "Doesn't take long with two of us, does it? How did you scratch your face?"

"I ran into a tree."

Harmony giggled. "I was always doing stuff like that when I was your age."

I don't think so.

Jesse peeked at Brian. He held his cell phone to his ear. Was he calling the number she had given him? If so, she hoped Liam sounded like a dad, and not a grouchy weirdo.

She studied the posters on the wall. There was everything from serious posters about saving whales to a framed cartoon of someone saving belly-button lint to recycle for cushion stuffing.

"Peace First has groups all over the world." Harmony squeezed Jesse's arm. "It's so exciting. In three days we're holding a huge rally with thousands of people. Kingston Martin is flying in to speak."

Jesse recognized the name. Kingston Martin was famous. He had survived a violent youth in his home country, spent time in prison, then become a peace activist. Was it simply chance that Ari and Josef were in this city at the same time? Kingston Martin was known to be tough and aggressive about his views. He made people angry. *Strange for a peace activist,* thought Jesse.

"Who's that?" Jesse pointed to a framed photograph of a gray-haired woman in old-fashioned clothes. She had one arm raised, with her fist clenched. The photo was crinkled on one corner where moisture had gathered under the glass.

"That's Fred. Frederica Gordon, actually. The founder of Peace First." Harmony's voice was hushed. "She's old now. Lives at Hillview Retirement Home. She's . . . well . . .

she forgets things. I visit her sometimes. People from all over the world ask about her when they call in. She says she's coming to the rally if she has to crawl. She plans to speak to the crowd. It would mean so much to everyone."

Jesse tried to look impressed. "Truly? From all over the world?"

Harmony laughed, her black lips a vivid contrast to her white teeth. "Sure. We had two journalists in here yesterday from some obscure country."

"Cool. Which paper did they work for?"

"Uh . . ." Harmony scratched her head. "They were freelancers. They sell their stories to anyone who wants to buy them."

"Did they take photos, too?"

A small frown separated Harmony's eyebrows. "No, they didn't. Maybe they were radio journalists."

Jesse's suspicions grew stronger.

Harmony shrugged. "Anyway, they spoke to Brian, made a couple of phone calls, and hung around the office long enough to eat most of our food, then left." She checked that Brian wasn't watching, then leaned forward to whisper to Jesse, "One of them was really cranky. I wanted to swat flies with his face."

"That bad, huh?"

"And talk about eaters! I thought I'd bought enough tandoori to feed all of us, but then these two showed up. I wasn't sure whether they were people or cement mixers."

Jesse grinned, encouraging Harmony to keep talking.

"Actually, the friendly one was kind of good-looking . . . for an old guy. He had a cute little scar above one eye."

Jesse's pulse raced. *Ari!*

10.

Shortly afterward, Jesse left the office and headed downtown. At a safe distance, she dropped her bundle of flyers into a trash can: "Sorry, Harmony." She felt slightly guilty, but there were plenty more flyers back at the office. Her C2 assignment was to find Ari, urgently.

The crossing sign turned red. Jesse stopped and checked her watch. Liam should already be waiting at their agreed meeting place. It had taken her longer in the Peace First office than she'd expected. Harmony talked a lot, but revealed only a little.

In the museum parking lot to Jesse's left,

a bus engine rattled to life. It was packed with excited students in yellow T-shirts. Jesse watched them jumping up and down as though their seats were on springs. There would be lots of noise inside that bus, chattering and laughter. For a moment, Jesse imagined herself in the middle of the chaos, like a normal kid.

The bus drew out of the parking lot and moved next to where Jesse and the others were waiting to cross.

She watched the faces pressed against the glass. These kids had lives that were very different from hers. Did they go home after school and play on their computers or with their friends? Did their parents offer them toast or cookies if they were hungry?

One face along the near side of the bus was turned away. Something about the shape of that head was familiar. Jesse looked more carefully.

Then he turned toward her.

Just for a second, Jesse had a clear view. She gasped. Pins and needles shot across her skin. She stood, unable to move or cry out.

Everything around her slowed down but the bus. Its left turn signal flicked on. The bus accelerated and pulled out onto the street.

At last, she found her voice. "Stop!" Ignoring the surprised faces around her, she began to run.

"Wait!" She waved her hands.

No one on the bus responded.

She tore along the sidewalk, her backpack thumping against her spine.

Another crossing sign turned red. A stream of traffic poured around the corner, blocking her path.

The bus turned right onto the highway, merged into the traffic, and was gone.

II.

Liam parked in front of Hillview Retirement Home, but kept the motor running. "My contacts have heard nothing. I'll check out accommodations, try to discover where Ari and Josef are staying. You find out if this old woman, Frederica Gordon, knows anything. She's more likely to open up to a young girl than a crusty guy like me. Text message me when you're finished."

Jesse found it hard to concentrate. The face at the bus window kept flashing before her eyes.

"You OK?" he asked.

Jesse jumped. "Sure."

He grunted. "Still mad at me about the training session?"

She dragged her thoughts back to Liam. She could not confide in him.

He laced his fingers together on top of the steering wheel. "If I'd refused to take you for training, Granger would have sent someone else. Someone who didn't care if you failed. Someone who might *want* you to fail. Believe me, you're better off with me. I had the van brought as close as possible. I kept an eye on you through binoculars."

Jesse looked over at him. "What would you have done if the dogs had caught up to me?"

"I'm glad it didn't come to that." He gave a small shrug. "Jesse, I look out for you as much as I can."

"Why do you work for C2?" she asked, suddenly anxious to know.

Liam stared straight ahead. "When I joined, I was young. I thought it would be something different, an adventure. I didn't realize what I was getting into. By the time I did, I'd also learned enough to know they wouldn't allow me to leave. I knew too much."

Jesse thought of Rohan.

"Being in C2 is like being caught in a stampede," added Liam. "All you can do is keep your balance, be wary, and try not to fall. Because if you do, you'll be crushed."

12.

The front doors of the retirement home opened into the TV room. Five residents in wheelchairs were lined up as though they were about to race for an invisible finish line. Two women shuffled about in fluffy slippers. A large TV in the corner broadcast a daytime soap opera. The volume was loud enough to hurt Jesse's ears. But it still wasn't enough to make the residents watch. Some stared down at the floor, others into space.

A woman in a navy dress approached Jesse. She was so thin that she seemed to be the same width from her head to the floor. Her puckered mouth folded around yellowed teeth. "May I help you, dear?"

"I'm looking for Frederica Gordon."

The woman pointed down the hallway. "Fred's in the dining room, at a birthday party." She whispered behind her bony hand. "*I'm* not invited. Not that I'd go, anyway. They're having alcohol. I haven't touched it since I was eighteen. Signed a pledge to abstain. Mind you, the staff only give them baby drinks. Hardly enough to wet their whistle."

"Thank you." Jesse followed the sounds of chatter and the chink of forks on plates to the dining room.

As she neared the doorway, a reedy female voice screeched, "No! Don't touch that!"

Jesse halted.

Other voices exploded into a babble of sound.

Cautiously, Jesse peered around the doorframe. A dozen men and women sat around a rectangular table. An elderly woman in a lilac dress with a lace collar leaped to her feet. She held a large orange in one hand. Although the woman had aged since the photograph was taken, Jesse recognized her as Frederica Gordon.

"Don't drink that wine, Harold!" repeated Fred.

A man with a magnificent white moustache laughed disparagingly.

Suddenly, Fred pitched the orange like a baseball. It knocked the wine glass from Harold's hand, smashing it onto the floor. "It'll poison you!"

13.

A burly man in white trousers and a white shirt stepped forward and took Fred by the arm. "Calm down, now."

Impatiently, Fred tried to shake off his hold, but failed. His hand was broad and strong, while her arm was spindly.

"*Coprinus atramentarius,*" Fred shouted. "I saw it on the kitchen sink when I went to sponge off this spot on my dress."

Jesse looked at Harold's plate. Suddenly she knew what was going on. She held up one hand. "Excuse me."

The elderly diners ignored her.

Harold stared down at his lost wine with outrage.

Without wasting more time on words, Jesse raised one hand and brought it down hard, in a karate chop, on the nearest plate. It snapped in halves.

Instantly, the voices hushed.

"Sorry. Fly on the plate," said Jesse. "They walk all over the food. Their taste buds are on their feet." She looked directly at Harold. "Have you just eaten mushrooms?"

He blustered, his red nose standing out like a beacon against his white moustache, "What's that got to do with anything? One of the volunteers brought them in. They were delicious."

"*She* knows." Fred smiled.

"If you eat mushrooms called *Coprinus atramentarius,* commonly known as inky caps, then have alcohol, you'll be sick," explained Jesse. "You get tingling, flushing, and rapid heartbeat."

The woman seated next to Harold pushed her glass away.

"Quite right," said Fred. "And he's got a bad heart. Why give it a nudge?" She frowned at him. "Although after the way you've spoken to me this afternoon, I'm tempted not to accept your apology."

Harold looked indignant. "I haven't made any apology."

"You will," said Fred, with quiet determination.

The man in the white shirt let go of Fred's arm. She sent him a disdainful glare, then another to Harold.

"Come, my dear." Fred waved Jesse toward her. "Let's go to my room. We have things to discuss. By the way, have you all met my granddaughter?"

14.

Jesse followed Fred along the hallway. Fred's shoes made an odd clicking sound on the tiles. She stopped and opened a door.

Instinctively, Jesse looked right. Movement? A shadow? Something had caught her attention. But what?

"Come in." Fred held the door open, waiting.

Jesse hesitated, then moved forward. It was probably nothing. Hillview Retirement Home was full of people. It would be odd if it had been totally quiet. And the shouting from the dining room would have attracted attention.

Fred's room was a surprise. The bedspread

and armchair were deep purple. They over-whelmed the small space, making it seem more like a cave than a room in a retirement home.

After closing the door, Fred leaned for-ward and sniffed Jesse's armpit.

Jesse jumped. "What are you doing?"

"You can lie with your lips, but not your pits," said Fred. "I traveled a lot when I was young. On one Pacific island, the locals sniffed armpits to detect people's true feelings. You, for example, are nervous."

Hello! You just stuck your nose in my arm-pit. What did you expect?

"Sit on this ducky stool."

Ducky? Any duck in that shade of purple would need a vet. Immediately. Jesse sat gin-gerly, ready to flee if Fred became too weird.

"Don't worry. I know you're not my grand-daughter." Fred smiled. "Skye has long, shiny black hair. Yours is mousy. I just wanted to rub their hairy old noses in it by saying I had family visiting when they didn't." She picked at the skin around her fingernail. A small strip of pale skin began to grow like an unrav-eling thread.

"Do you see your granddaughter often?"

"I never approved of my daughter, you know. No backbone."

Does she mean Skye's mother? "You have a daughter?" asked Jesse.

A puzzled expression swept Fred's face. "I do? What's her name?"

See if she knows anything, Liam had said. That was probably impossible. Even if Fred did know of Ari or Josef, she wouldn't remember it. Her mind flopped all over the place.

Fred touched Jesse's face. "You're wounded."

"It's nothing."

Absentmindedly, Fred scratched Jesse's head as though she were a pet dog. Her fingernails were long, but her touch was gentle. "I do this for Skye."

Jesse sat tensely, uncertain whether to move away or sit still.

"Why are you here?" demanded Fred.

Jesse's eyes popped wide open. Her voice, when she spoke, was slightly breathless. "I'm volunteering at Peace First and I wanted to meet you. You're a hero."

Fred blew a raspberry with her lips.

"You must have lots of visitors who want to meet the woman who started Peace First."

Fred said nothing.

"Have you had many visitors this week?" asked Jesse.

"I'm not sure. Sometimes I can't remember things. . . ."

Jesse shrugged. Maybe Ari and Josef had only pretended to be interested in Fred to conceal their real motive. *Why make contact with an old woman who throws oranges and can't remember her own daughter?*

"Anyone who knows *Coprinus atramentarius* has a lot going for her. I like you." Fred's blue eyes flashed. "I know a secret and I'll tell you what it is."

15.

Liam and Jesse sat in the parked car and stared across the street at an empty church with a FOR SALE sign. Graffiti was scrawled across the front doors, and the windows were boarded up.

"Are you sure this is correct?" asked Liam.

"This is the address Fred gave me. I wrote it down. She said there was a secret here."

"I'd bet my back teeth she was simply rambling."

"I thought they were fake."

"What?"

"Your teeth."

Liam rolled his eyes.

"When Ari and Josef visited Peace First, they asked about Fred," said Jesse.

"Five minutes. Then we're out of here. We have to check it out, but I don't think it will lead anywhere. But, just in case, be careful. This would be a good place for someone to hide. I'll go left. You take the right side."

Jesse looked again at the old church. Were Ari and Josef in there, peering out at them?

She slipped from the car, edged across the street, then along the sidewalk till she reached the front of the church. Shaggy bushes, still alive in what was left of the garden, gave her some protection.

Liam slid one hand under his jacket, ready to pull out his gun. Jesse didn't have one. Didn't want one. Yet her hands felt empty, vulnerable. Still, she had her tae kwon do and karate. And if all else failed, she could run fast.

As Liam disappeared around the corner, Jesse crept along the path, her hands touching the stone wall. There were no doors on this side. She checked behind her, then in front. The boarded windows showed no sign of being tampered with. Wooden slats were firmly secured over them all. Anyway, given how high up the windows were, they would be difficult to climb through.

She stood still and listened. There was no sound, apart from the wind whistling through the boards on the windows and the hum of car engines from the main road not far away.

Her heart beat faster as she reached the corner and peeked around it. Liam appeared a second later. He shook his head. All clear.

At the rear of the church they found a small cemetery. Jesse imagined the real estate agent bragging about what a bargain it was, if you ignored fifty bodies in the backyard.

"I never knew this was here," said Liam. "It's completely surrounded by apartments."

Jesse walked among the headstones. Some were old and damaged; others looked reasonably new. Had her parents been buried in a place like this after their car crash? Had C2 taken care of the funeral? They had adopted Jesse. Maybe they had organized everything else, too.

"The old woman's a fruit loop." Liam sighed. "Let's go."

"Wait!" She pointed to a damaged head-stone. "Look."

The vandals had been busy out here, too. A vase of red roses had been knocked over. The flowers were only just beginning to wilt. The name carved in the stone was *Skye Gordon.* She had died eight years earlier, when she was twenty. The list of those who missed her included her grand-mother — Frederica Gordon — and Jogger. *Is that a pet's name?* Some words were missing, along with the right side of the headstone. But Jesse could still read *Killed in the service of others.*

Jesse looked down at the grave. Poor Fred. Her granddaughter had been impor-tant to her and she wanted Jesse to know it. But maybe it wasn't that simple. Was Fred trying to warn her about something?

She stooped to tuck the sad, wilted flow-ers back into their vase. She couldn't leave them dying on the bare ground.

Jesse looked up. For a second she stared, without understanding, at a red dot between Liam's shoulder blades. Then she launched forward, wrapped her arms around his legs and tackled him to the ground. He hit it hard.

Something cracked into the headstone beside them. A wedge of stone flew backward, like a head being parted from a body.

16.

"Liam!" Jesse grabbed his jacket and shook him. "Someone's shooting at us."

Liam screamed. "My shoulder!"

A second bullet whizzed between them and hit the ground. A puff of dust danced up in response.

"Take cover!" A white monument stood over the next grave. It was large enough to provide shelter. "Behind the angel."

Groaning, Liam squirmed forward on his stomach. Jesse scrambled on her hands and knees. She sat, wedged close to Liam, her back against the monument. Then she tucked in her elbows and drew her knees into her body, making a smaller target.

Another bullet ricocheted off a metal plaque on the church wall.

"Never thought I'd be saved by an angel." Liam looked up at the tall buildings surrounding the small churchyard. "The sniper could be in any one of those apartments."

Ping. Another shot blew dust from the monument into Jesse's face, making her cough.

"We can't stay here. We have to get to the car." Beads of perspiration dotted Liam's forehead. "You've dislocated my shoulder, thumb sucker."

Jesse felt tempted to dislocate the other one. "I saved you from getting shot."

He nodded. "There *is* that."

She wriggled uncomfortably and pulled a squashed can from under her thigh. There were papers, cans, and bottles scattered around the cemetery. *Zing.* And bullets. A bottle lay on its side beside the next headstone, and it was still half full.

"Do you smoke?" she asked, pretty sure that he didn't. She'd never smelled smoke on him.

"No. It's bad for your health. Mind you, so

is getting shot at. What sort of question is that when someone's trying to kill us?"

"We'll have to do this the hard way, then. I'll be back in a minute." Jesse took a deep breath, counted to three, then dived across the open space between the headstones.

17.

Jesse grabbed the bottle, unscrewed the cap, and sniffed. "Phew." Her eyes watered. *Perfect.*

Behind the angel, Liam stared across at her. His eyes were so wide they seemed to have doubled in size.

"Catch," called Jesse. In case she didn't make it back, Liam would have the bottle. She pitched it straight and fast. *Zing.* A bullet between the headstones showed that the sniper was watching closely, Liam caught the bottle with one hand, then cried out in pain.

Can I make it back? The smaller headstone wasn't enough protection. Silently, she crossed her fingers and once again counted to three.

As she leaped back beside Liam, she felt something sting the back of her foot. She thumped back into place.

Liam groaned.

"Sorry. I was in a hurry." She checked her foot. There was a furrow across the back of her sneaker. Another inch and that last bullet would have taken off her heel.

"Give me your tie," she commanded Liam as she reached for the bottle.

He obeyed without argument. *He really must be in pain.* With trembling fingers, Jesse unscrewed the bottle cap once more and slipped the end of the tie into the bottle.

"Ah ha," said Liam. "A distraction."

Jesse looked about for twigs to rub together. She needed a spark.

"Here." With his good hand, Liam dug in the inside pocket of his jacket and pulled out a pen. He twisted it and a spark ignited.

"Mm. Cool gadget. I want one of those." Jesse grabbed it and held the tiny flame to the tie. It took only a few seconds to begin burning.

"Natural fibers," said Liam. "Wow. That's an expensive tie."

"Ready?"

Liam nodded.

Her heart pounded. She had to wait till just the right moment. Throw it too soon and the flames might go out. Wait too long and there would be two barbecued agents.

"Now!" she whispered fiercely through clenched teeth, and hurled the bottle. It exploded into a ball of flames as it broke.

Using the flames and smoke as cover, they ran along the row of headstones and around the corner of the church. Another bullet hit the wall as they turned. Whoever was shooting at them had been distracted for only a few seconds. But it might be enough. Now he would have to change position.

Unexpectedly, Liam halted.

"What's the matter?" asked Jesse.

He swayed like a reed in a breeze.

Please don't faint. She had done weight training in the C2 gym, but she couldn't lift an unconscious Liam.

"I need this arm to change gears," he said. "I can't drive."

18.

Liam fumbled with one hand to do up his seat belt, then threw a desperate look at Jesse. "Are you sure about this?"

"You pick. Either I drive or we both get shot to pieces." She turned the key. The motor started, making the steering wheel vibrate faintly under her hands.

"OK. You win."

"I know what to do. I've seen you drive."

A bullet tore through the back window and smacked into the floor behind them. Glass showered over the back seat.

"Go, go, go!" bellowed Liam.

Jesse shoved her foot on the accelerator and changed gears. The car hopped as if it had the hiccups. *Maybe this isn't as easy as it looks.*

A white van came toward them on the other side of the road. Jesse's hands tightened on the wheel. *Is this someone coming in for a closer shot?*

Liam's car jerked again. The van passed them and disappeared around a corner. The driver had not even glanced in their direction.

"Change gears," said Liam.

"I know." Jesse's voice was just as loud as his. *Come on, Betsy.*

"Watch out for the curb!"

Jesse pushed her foot on the accelerator and the car sped up.

"Calm. Let's be calm. We can both do this. Aaah . . ." Liam cried out in pain as Jesse stopped suddenly at an intersection.

He took a deep breath. "Turn left. It'll take us to the highway. . . . We can blend in. You're doing fine."

Jesse glanced at the rearview mirror, then repositioned her hands on the wheel. *That's better. More comfortable.*

"Soon as we're out of range, we'll stop and

get a taxi," said Liam. "I'll come back for the car later."

The driver in the next car peered at their broken back window, then at Jesse. His curious glance grew into an open-mouthed gape.

"Try not to look so young," said Liam.

How do I do that?

"Don't wait for the light. Turn left. *Now!*" he ordered.

Liam's car surged across the intersection, veering left. *Oops. Too fast.* She braked. The back of the car spun out.

"Don't brake on a corner," said Liam. "Brake just before it. Drive around the corner so the tires grip properly. Accelerate gently as you straighten up." He put one hand behind him and rummaged among the litter. "Ah, here it is. You're drawing attention to us." Liam put a cap on her with one hand. "There. That'll shield your face."

Don't brake, change gears, don't look so young, cover your face. Was there anything Liam had left out?

"Don't you dare drive like this ordinarily." He shook his head. "What am I saying? You're not old enough to drive."

"It's an emergency. Besides, I'm a genius, remember?" Jesse felt as though a heavy brick sat in her stomach. Her armpits and palms were damp with sweat.

"Brake. *Brake!*" yelled Liam.

She missed the turning car in front by a tiny margin. "Sorry."

"Pull over now."

Jesse peered into the rearview mirror. "I don't think so."

"What do you mean *you don't think so?*"

"There's a car behind us."

"That's all right, Jesse. As long as you turn on your blinker, he'll see you."

Her nerves at fever pitch, she shouted, "I think we're being *followed!*"

Liam swung round to take a better look. "I seriously doubt that a plump mother with four children, fluffy dice hanging from the rearview mirror, and a dog with droopy ears are in the spy business. Besides, she's turning."

"I'm never driving another car. Ever."

He raised his eyebrows. "That's probably the least of your worries. We have to report to Granger that we can't find the target."

19.

Director Granger sat quietly, his hands folded neatly on the desk in front of him. Yet Jesse felt her stomach tighten. An undercurrent of menace radiated from him.

Liam, his arm held firmly in a sling, slouched in his chair, as though he was relaxed. But he continually tapped one foot on the carpet.

"You've returned without the target," said Granger with a lift of one eyebrow. "And injured."

"We were shot at," said Liam. "That's a good sign of progress."

It is? Jesse could think of better ones.

"We've stirred someone up," Liam added.

"And who might that be?"

Liam cleared his throat. "We're . . . investigating."

Which actually means we don't have a clue. "It shows we're on the right track," she said, supporting Liam.

"We're a lot further advanced than we were this morning," added Liam. "We know Ari and Josef went to Peace First and asked about the founder, Frederica Gordon. She sent us to the abandoned church, where we were targeted by the sniper."

"Have you interrogated her?"

A sick feeling rose in Jesse's throat. Had Liam interrogated people before? Had he killed anybody?

"No point, sir," added Liam. "The old woman's . . . er . . . she has dementia."

"I spent time with her today," said Jesse. "She can't remember her own children. She doesn't make sense."

"Right now, neither do you two," said Granger. "You were shot at by an unknown marksman while investigating a suspect who was already dead, having been sent there by an old woman with dementia." He shrugged.

"What I require is results. I don't care how you get them." He focused attention on Jesse. "It is *vital* that Ari is brought in, quickly."

Why is Granger staring at me in particular? Jesse thought of the familiar face she had glimpsed in the bus. The Director couldn't possibly know about that, could he? Instinctively, she wanted to turn away in case he read her expression. But she relaxed her facial muscles and kept eye contact.

Granger gestured toward the door.

Jesse stood.

"Liam, stay," said Granger.

She left the room with her mind working overtime. *What doesn't Granger want me to hear?*

20.

Back in her room, Jesse locked the door. She was eager to log on to her computer. But she mustn't be careless.

She dragged a chair across and propped it underneath the door handle, so that no one could turn it. Mary Holt had her own key and used it without thinking. From her secret hiding place, Jesse took a small scanner and checked the room for listening devices. All clear.

Now she could switch on her computer. She entered her fingerprints, and then her current four passwords, which she changed every day. Rohan had shown her how to set up a system that re-routed her e-mails and Web searches all around the world. Anyone who tried to electronically track her would fail.

Now, don't get your hopes up. But even as she tried to talk herself into being calm, her breathing quickened. She opened a search engine and typed in "Branwood School." They might not have a Web site, but it was worth a try. She felt as though something heavy pressed down on her chest.

The guide at the museum had been definite. Eyes watery with a cold, he had blown his nose on a checked handkerchief, making a sound like a squashed orange. "Yellow T-shirts? On a bus? That'd be Branwood. They visit every year. They do the round trip — the zoo, art gallery, our museum, and if they beg enough, KFC or McDonald's."

Jesse's computer screen displayed several sites that mentioned Branwood School. She chose the official one. The welcome page showed a photograph of a gray brick building boasting a cheerful sign.

A tingle ran through Jesse as she clicked through staff photos, artwork, writing competition results, special visitors to the school, the library. Sports day photos showed tousled boys and girls in shorts, displaying colored ribbons. So far, no face looked familiar. Science and Information Technology was the last section. There was text about student projects, then more photos.

Jesse stared. A sound like rushing water filled her ears. Two boys sat at computers, grinning for the camera. One of them had green eyes, a dimple in his chin, and a gap between his front teeth. His hair was longer than Jesse remembered, and had a side part. The caption gave his name as Peter Keaton.

It said the two boys had won a prize for a science project three months ago. That couldn't be right. He would not have been at Branwood then. He was at C2.

21.

A loud knock made Jesse jump. Immediately she switched off the computer. No one could see what was on that screen. No one. Moving swiftly, she dragged the chair back to its usual place and unlocked the door.

Liam stood there. His black sling blended into his dark shirt, creating the illusion that his arm was missing. "May I come in?" He rolled his eyes to indicate the surveillance cameras in the corridor.

Reluctantly, she stepped back.

Just as Jai always did, Liam followed the big blue footprints she had pasted to the floor. He sat on a wooden chair at her table. Jesse sat opposite.

"Do you want to talk about what happened in the churchyard today?" he asked.

She shook her head.

"Being shot at is an unpleasant experience. You might have nightmares."

So what's new? When her conscious mind was asleep, memories of the laboratory took over. Flashes of hypodermic needles, strange medical instruments, and dark rooms often disturbed her. Those people in white coats saw only an experiment and not a child.

Jesse longed to ask what Liam and the Director had talked about behind closed doors. Did Liam look uncomfortable or was it just her imagination?

"I checked yesterday's phone records from Peace First," he said. "They're whipping up enthusiasm for the protest march. Most calls were to the media. No point protesting if no one knows about it. I ran a background check on the people in the Peace First office. Brian Marinelli turned out to be a surprise. He was once engaged to Skye Gordon, the old woman's granddaughter."

"Really?"

"They both worked for an international aid agency overseas. Brian, it seems, had an usual nickname back then. . . ."

"Jogger."

He nodded. "Brownie point to you. You guessed it. Apparently, Brian jogged every morning before work."

Jesse struggled with the idea of Brian jogging.

"He was injured in the same bomb blast that killed Skye."

That explains his lopsided face.

"There was also a call from Peace First to a city hotel. You can check it out tomorrow. Be ready to leave at seven. I have other leads to follow tonight."

"You're not going to . . . interrogate Fred, are you?"

He shook his head.

Would his answer be different if Fred's memory were intact?

"You're not needed tonight. Apparently Granger thinks kids need a thing called sleep."

That made Granger sound almost human. It must have been a mistake. "Whoever shot at us today saw what I look like. Should I wear a disguise tomorrow?"

"Be safer. Make up a cover story and dress to match it. The Supply Department will fix you up."

Jesse nodded, but worry gnawed at her. Was Fred more than she appeared to be? Was her dementia real or an act? Jesse liked Fred. But the old woman had given her an address and, shortly afterward, someone had shot at them. Were they followed, or had Fred given the information to someone else?

22.

Awkwardly, Jesse maneuvered her crutches across the polished tiles of the hotel foyer. Already her armpits were sore from leaning on the handles. A woman with woolly hair walked past and gave her a sympathetic look.

The public phones on one wall beckoned like magnets. Jesse dragged her eyes away from them. No time now. Her call would have to wait.

Passing the sofas and the rack of international newspapers, she moved slowly toward the hotel desk. She glimpsed her reflection in the shiny elevator doors. *Even I feel sorry for me.* Her left leg was heavily bandaged. Hints of purple around her right eye suggested bruising. There was a second bandage wrapped around her left hand. Her black beanie was pulled down low, level with her eyebrows. *What would Jai say if he could see me now?*

A young man in hotel uniform took a step toward her, hesitated, then stepped back. Jesse kept one eye on him. After yesterday's surprise attack in the graveyard, she was doubly sensitive. But it seemed the young man was going to offer help, then changed his mind. *Good. There isn't much he could do, apart from carrying me. And that isn't going to happen.*

She reached the counter.

A woman with gray streaks in her hair smiled uncertainly. Her badge read MARILYN. "How may I help you, dear?"

The "dear" was a good sign.

Jesse sniffed. "I want to ask about someone who's staying here. At least, I think he's staying here."

A man in a navy suit barged between Jesse and Marilyn. "Messages?" he asked in a brash voice.

Marilyn gave him the smile of a crocodile

who wants to grab its prey, drag it to the bottom of a murky river, and roll it over till it stops breathing. "No, Mr. Burton. No messages."

He grunted and stalked out the front door as though it were Marilyn's fault that no one had contacted him. Jesse understood perfectly why he had no messages. He had the manners of a starving pig.

She coughed to regain Marilyn's attention. "I don't know what name he's using, but I think my dad's staying here." Her voice cracked on the word *dad*. She hadn't planned that. It just happened. *It would be so exciting to ask, for real, for my dad and find him waiting.*

Marilyn shook her head. "I really can't give out information about our guests."

"Dad's hiding. He left Mom and me because he feels bad. But we want him back." Jesse gave a wan smile. "I need to persuade Dad to come home. You see, there was this car accident . . ."

Tell a story that's close to the truth, Liam had told her. *Then you'll find it easy to remember and you'll sound genuine.* Maybe. But

Jesse felt as though she was telling Marilyn about her real father.

"Dad was driving and we hit a tree. I was hurt. Dad feels so bad. I need to find him and tell him it wasn't his fault."

Marilyn's brow crinkled like a potato chip. "But if you don't know what name he's using, how can I tell you if he's here? Even if I was allowed to — which I'm *not*."

Jesse leaned one elbow on the counter and dug into her new shoulder bag. She pulled out a photo of Ari and pushed it across the counter.

Marilyn made no move to pick up the photo, but she looked at it. "I haven't seen him. He might have checked in when I wasn't on duty. There are many guests here."

Jesse dabbed at her eyes with a crumpled tissue.

"Don't cry." Marilyn put one hand to her chest. "Tell you what, the ones who know what's really going on are the cleaners. My friend Ruth is on duty today. Why don't we ask her?"

Before Marilyn could say more, a noisy bunch of tourists wearing identical red caps flooded through the front doors. Jesse recognized their language as Spanish. The young man in uniform rushed to help with their suitcases. He'd be there for a while. A large bus was parked outside and more visitors were still coming.

"Look, it's about to become chaotic at the desk," said Marilyn. "Can you manage going up to the fourth floor? Ruth's up there. Tell her I sent you."

Jesse rewarded her with a grateful smile, but Marilyn's attention had already switched to the tourists.

So far, so good. Although the hard part would be dealing with Ari if she actually found him.

23.

Alone in the elevator, Jesse leaned on the crutches and looked down at the floor. With the beanie over her hair and no clear view of her face, she would be hard to identify on the security cameras.

The elevator door opened with an electronic *ping*. A falsely cheerful recorded voice said, "Have a nice day." Jesse rolled her eyes. She hopped into the empty corridor. From the far end came the hum of a vacuum cleaner and muffled voices. Although Jesse was tempted to ditch the crutches and walk naturally, she resisted. It would take longer to negotiate the corridor, but it was safer to keep up her pretense.

She stopped in the open doorway of a guest room. It had two double beds and wide windows with a pretty view of the botanical gardens. A tall woman was dusting the bedside tables. Sounds from the bathroom suggested that there was a second person in there.

"Excuse me," Jesse called in a loud voice. "Is Ruth here?"

A second woman, round-faced and bright-eyed, came out of the bathroom carrying a cleaning cloth. In one swift glance, she took in Jesse's bedraggled appearance, then pretended she hadn't noticed. "Yes?"

Jesse repeated the story she had told Marilyn down stairs, then showed the photograph of Ari.

Ruth shook her head. "No, haven't seen him. What about you, Margie?" She showed her companion, who also shook her head. "Sorry. I hope you find him."

Jesse felt a mixture of emotions — disappointment that the search wasn't over, but relief that she didn't have to detain the man just yet. She thanked the two women and hobbled from the room. Their eyes would be following her, she guessed.

Back in the empty corridor, she hesitated. The important information often came after the official conversation.

"Poor kid." Margie's voice drifted through the open doorway. "Don't reckon she'll see that dad of hers again."

Jesse found a STAFF ONLY door across the corridor. She turned the handle, but it was locked. It took only a few seconds to take a metal pin from her bag and insert it in the lock. The door swung open. *Piece of cake.* She ducked inside, leaving the door slightly ajar. It smelled musty. There were shelves stacked with linen, and a spare vacuum cleaner sat on the carpet. Jesse put her ear to the space between the door and the door frame.

"Wonder if that kid's mother knows she's here?"

"Don't know. Maybe she sent her. Some mothers have a lot to answer for."

"It was the father who ran away. Running away never solved anything."

Sometimes it might. Jesse imagined herself and Jai walking away from C2 with packed bags in their hands. The trouble was, she could only imagine that scene with the terror that would come from knowing they would be hunted down.

"The king suite is next. That bigwig from overseas is in there. . . . can't think of his name . . ."

"Sam Smith, the room chart says."

"That's not his real name." The sound of a vacuum cleaner cord being retracted came next. "None of the famous ones check in under their real names. Otherwise their fans and the media drive them nuts. Just a reminder because you're new, Margie. Don't ask for his autograph. Not that you'll get a chance. He's surrounded by staff — bodyguards, yoga teacher, massage therapist, even a hairdresser. Don't know why he bothers. He's going bald. Maybe she polishes his scalp."

"That's a worry. My dad used to *spit* on his shoes to polish them."

Muffled giggles followed.

"He's that peace activist," said Ruth. "You've seen him on TV. Kingston Martin."

Jesse bit her lip. *That's interesting.* Josef, a professional killer, had called the hotel where Kingston Martin was staying. Ari and Josef had visited Peace First. Martin was speaking at their rally. It was too much to be a coincidence. Did Josef plan to kill Kingston Martin?

The *ping* of the elevator told Jesse that the doors had opened on this floor. The heavy footsteps of several people headed closer. She eased the door almost shut, cutting off her view, but she could still listen. Barely.

Someone stopped right outside the STAFF ONLY door. A male voice spoke with authority. "Our contact said she's on this floor. Start from the end and check every room. Don't let her escape. Remember, the crutches are part of a disguise."

24.

Jesse eased the door shut. *Please don't squeak.* Gently, she turned the lock. That would delay them only for a few seconds. It was an easy lock to pick. Besides, the cleaners would have keys.

She hurried to the window, but it was bolted shut and there was no balcony or ledge.

Voices in the corridor outside set Jesse's heart racing.

What about going up? No, that wouldn't work. Not only was the air-conditioning vent far too small, it was close to heavy shelving.

I could wait till they open the door, then fight my way out. Jesse was a master at tae kwon do and good at karate, too. But even so, a bunch of big men with even bigger muscles had the advantage. If they carried weapons, and she bet they did, she would have even less chance.

Her throat constricted, making it hard to swallow. Then she thought of Jai. She had promised to return.

And what about the familiar face on the bus? She must find out the truth.

Turning from left to right, she took a second, more careful look. *There had to be a way.* Her pupils enlarged as she focused on a door, a two-foot square in the wall. A fragment of cloth protruded from one corner. She tugged at the handle and the little door opened into the room. A pillowcase that had been caught in a hinge wafted down the metal slide, out of sight. *It's a chute for dirty linen.* It would go down to the laundry room.

Jesse poked her head into the space in the wall. This was the fourth floor. What if there was nothing at the end to soften her fall? *If I crash onto a hard surface, I'll need these bandages for real.* Although it might be possible to ease down the chute, with her back propped against one wall and her feet against the other. She had done something similar once before.

The voices outside grew louder.

Urgently, Jesse grabbed a clean sheet, wrapped it around the crutches, and dropped them down the chute. Otherwise, they would give away that she'd been in the room.

She balanced in a sitting position on the edge of the chute. Her legs dangled into darkness.

Muffled sounds indicated that the padded crutches had arrived downstairs.

A key rattled in the lock.

25.

Inside the dark chute, Jesse's back was pressed hard against one wall, her feet jammed against the other.

Then her feet slipped. Instinctively, she opened her mouth to scream, then clamped it shut. Suddenly she was falling — down, down into darkness.

Her hand scraped a rough joint, then her elbow. She tightened her arms against her sides, pinning her shoulder bag firmly, straightened her legs, and rode the slope as though it were a giant slippery slide.

Confused, she was aware of a flash of light. Something soft covered and surrounded her.

Cobwebs. Even as she thought it, she knew it couldn't be.

With a muffled *whoomph,* she landed. Her head was covered. She couldn't see. Stunned, she took a minute to get her breath back. What was that under her leg? She felt to see what it was. *Oh, the crutch.*

It's just as well I brought a shoulder bag today and not the backpack. Otherwise it'd be rammed into my spine.

She lay still, a white haze around her. *Sheets.* The cobwebs were sheets. The flash of light had been someone opening another door to the chute. *I've fallen into a large laundry bag.*

Boots clomped on the floor. Voices. A cough. Still dizzy and trembling, Jesse tried to concentrate.

"You take the back door," a man said. "That'll be every entrance sealed."

Jesse didn't recognize the voice. Was this Ari or Josef? Ari's English was supposed to be just about perfect. The file had said nothing about Josef's language skills.

Slowly, gently, she pushed aside the sheet

that covered her face. All she could see was the back of the man's head. His shaved scalp gleamed. His neck was thick and powerful-looking. When he turned slightly, she glimpsed a large nose, bent like a beak. She did not recognize him.

"Hey!"

Jesse gasped.

The second voice, also male, added, "The van driver wants to go."

Another pile of linen dropped from the chute, burying Jesse deeper.

"Check the van before it leaves. Bring that nosy kid to me. I want to find out what she knows."

"Then what?"

"We make sure she won't talk to any-one else."

"She's just a kid."

The man in authority snorted. "No one is *just* anything. Remember our purpose. Everything must go smoothly at the rally tomorrow. She's history. What does one indi-vidual matter? The kid could interfere. We have to get rid of her."

26.

Before she could decide what to do, she felt movement. The bag tilted. Sounds from above her, and the sudden darkness, told her the top of the bag had been closed.

She half-rolled left, then right. Then came rumbling from beneath, and vibrations.

"One more, Larry," a voice called. It wasn't either of the men searching for her.

Her stomach whirled as the bag was lifted upward. She held her breath, waiting for someone to complain about the strange heaviness of the bag. But it didn't happen. Maybe they used machinery to lift.

Suddenly she was dumped on a hard

surface. Although the linen around her was some protection, the landing still jarred.

She heard footsteps. Doors slammed. The van motor started.

Jesse listened carefully for sounds that might identify the route that the van was taking. A police or ambulance siren flashed past and faded, then there was the deep roar of a truck.

It was hot inside the bag. She felt tangled, surrounded. Perspiration soaked her armpits and back. Her chest was tight. Eyelids drooping, she felt a wave of dizziness sweep her brain. *I'm so tired.* Then awareness pierced her befuddled thoughts. *There isn't enough air. I'm suffocating.*

Jesse dug in her bag for her pocketknife.

Feeling through a jumble of sheets, she reached the canvas wall of the bag. She stabbed at it, piercing the fabric. It wouldn't slit easily, but she kept hacking at it. *Too bad if anyone's in the back of the van when I leap out.*

Like a moth emerging from a cocoon, she squeezed her body out of the laundry bag into the fresher air of the van. She took a deep breath and looked around. The back part of the van was stacked with green canvas bags like the one she had just ruined with her pocketknife. Fortunately, there was a metal partition between her and the driver. He could not see her.

Jesse took off her beanie and shoved it and the knife into her bag. With both hands, she fluffed her hair into reasonable order.

What's that? She jumped. Something thin and dark stuck to the bandage on her leg. Then she grinned, plucked off a lost sock and tossed it into the corner of the van.

Swiftly, she unwound the useless bandages and used them to wipe the makeup from her face. Amazing how a little purple here and a touch of black there had made her look bruised and battered. Leaving the crutches inside the bag, she stuffed the spilled sheets back and turned the split to the back wall. If everything looked normal when the driver opened the door, it would buy her some time.

There were double doors at the back of the van, but with no handles on the inside.

She pushed at the doors. They didn't budge. She tried to fiddle the lock with the metal pin she had used on the door at the hotel. That didn't work, either. She considered kicking the doors open. But they were too solid. Besides, the noise would alert the driver to an intruder. She was stuck till someone opened the doors from the outside.

The van stopped

Jesse dived for cover.

27.

The double doors were flung open. Light invaded the back of the van. Jesse prepared to push the driver and bolt, if he spotted her. But he retreated, leaving the doors open.

She crawled to the doors and peered out. They were parked at the back of what looked like a small hospital. *He's collecting more laundry.* She slipped from the van, then headed for a row of thick shrubs.

Even if the driver reappeared, Jesse looked different from the badly injured victim on crutches. There was a spring in her step, a smile on her open face, an eagerness to take in everything around her. She'd learned that just a few gestures could suggest an entirely different personality.

But she still half-expected a sudden ruckus. Only when she mingled with the pedestrians did she feel safer.

Jesse sauntered casually. Inside her head, she heard Liam's voice. *Don't run unless you have to. It draws attention. Blend in.*

The gentle breeze cooled her face. She breathed in deeply, delighted to be free of the van.

Cautiously, she stopped in front of a shop window. The glass provided a good mirror. She could see behind her without appearing to look. People seemed to be going about their own business quite happily. Even a dog asleep on the sidewalk simply yawned as she passed.

Soon she could message Liam to pick her up. But not yet. She had something else to do. This was her big chance and she wasn't about to lose it. She entered a small shopping center and found a public phone tucked away in the back corner. Silently, she thanked Liam for the allowance.

She dialed the number she had memorized. It began to ring.

When she had imagined herself making this call, she had not considered that there would be no answer. *What if they can't hear the phone? What if they're having a day off?*

Disappointment squeezed her like a living creature with multiple arms.

28.

"Good morning, Branwood School. Rachel speaking." The voice from the phone made Jesse jump.

She couldn't speak for a second. Then, pitching her voice lower than usual, she said, "My name is Jessica Ashford." It always felt strange using another name, as though she was wearing someone else's clothes. "I'm on the committee of the Science Foundation. One of your students, Peter Keaton, has won a prize in our current competition."

"Oh, how wonderful!" The receptionist's tone suggested that she liked the boy.

"May I speak to him please?"

"He's in class right now."

"I need to check that this work was all his own, that no one helped him. Then we can mail him his prize."

Jesse waited. In situations like this, the first to speak usually gave in.

"Oh . . . I suppose it would be all right," The receptionist was flustered. "Will you hold while I get him?"

"Certainly." *I mustn't get my hopes up.* But Jesse had seen the photograph. There were so many questions to ask. Most of them would wait till they arranged to meet. Branwood was quite a distance, but she was determined.

She heard the rattle of someone picking up the phone. "H . . . hello? This is P . . . Peter."

Her heart skipped. "Hi. It's Jesse here."

Instead of the reaction she expected, he simply said, "You w . . . wanted to talk to me?"

"It's Jesse."

"What happened to the other p . . . person?"

"I tripped you when you were five and you split your finger and had six stitches.

Remember?" Her voice was tight with anxiety. "You still have the scar."

"I don't have a s . . . scar on my finger."

"Yes you *do*. On your right hand. The forefinger. Go on. *Look*. Why are you pretending you don't know me?" Jesse's voice was getting louder.

Why was Rohan stuttering? Was it part of a disguise, a new identity?

Persevering, she said, "Can't you talk with that woman listening? Is it dangerous?"

The receptionist's voice piped up in the background. "Is everything all right, Peter?"

"I th . . . think it's a crank call," he said, and hung up.

29.

Jesse strode into the bus depot. Ari would have to wait. Liam would have to wait. The whole world could wait. She didn't care. She was too close to give up on Rohan now. Why didn't he remember her? Had C2 wiped his memory? Had he been in an accident? Or, now that he was free of C2, was he afraid to talk to her? None of these ideas explained why he had no scar on his forefinger. *If* he was telling the truth.

She marched to the counter and made eye contact with the man behind it. He wore half-glasses, propped well down his nose, to read his newspaper. Three fatty chins disguised the real shape of his jaw. His bottom lip was shiny with saliva.

"Excuse me." Jesse smiled at him. "I think I left my bracelet on the bus yesterday. We went to the museum. Branwood School trip."

His chins wobbled as he opened a large drawer to his right. "Nope. No bracelet in lost and found." The tip of his tongue snaked out to lick his bottom lip.

"I wore it on the bus. I'm certain," she whined, to make him feel sorry for her. "My mother gave it to me."

He pushed a form across the counter. "Fill this in." Then he went back to reading his newspaper.

"If I could just take a look . . ."

"You need proof of ownership," he added without looking up. "And bring a responsible adult back with you."

Jesse turned on her heel and left the office.

She walked around the block, found the back gate, and went in.

The bus she had seen was a shabby silver one with the destination — LOST — marked humorously on the front. The registration number was imprinted on her mind.

She hid by a Dumpster and checked out the line of parked buses. The one she wanted wasn't there. She hoped that it hadn't been booked for another tour.

Music blared from inside a large shed. She scuttled across the yard, avoiding a middle-aged man in navy overalls, then a young blonde woman.

The bus was parked in a shed. A young man with a goatee beard, also wearing overalls, whistled as he wrote on a clipboard.

"Dale!" came a voice from the yard.

Jesse dropped to the ground and wriggled close to the wheels of another bus. She watched the two men from her hiding place.

The middle-aged man in overalls pointed to the bus she was interested in. "Serviced forty-seven yet?"

"It's up next."

"The cleaners will be here in an hour. Get a move on. There's another six buses waiting."

Excellent. That means the one I want is untouched.

Dale flared his nostrils.

Thirty percent of the population does that. Jesse sighed. It would be so cool to forget the useless facts that stuck in her brain. An extraordinary memory was sometimes a real pain.

The older man retreated, leaving Dale to resume his scribbling and whistling. Jesse could see that number forty-seven had its doors open. But Dale was in the way.

Shall I take the time to win Dale over, or just knock him out? If she didn't check in soon, Liam would become impatient, perhaps suspicious.

Dale grabbed a stained mug from his workbench and headed in the opposite direction.

Coffee must be more urgent than the boss's nagging.

Jesse ran straight for the door of the bus. She bent double and scooted down the aisle. *Row ten. This is where Rohan sat.* Jesse opened her bag and took out the items she had prepared. Rohan had turned his head and grabbed the metal bar in front of him with both hands. She raised her hands without touching the bar. *Here. He put his fingers here.* She dipped a feather into a small container of ground pencil lead and dusted the bar. Right in front of her, on top of the other partial prints, was a perfect set of fingerprints.

Jesse took a roll of sticky tape from her bag. Working quickly, she pressed the tape over the fingerprints, and over several others nearby for comparison.

Off-key whistling told her that Dale was returning. Deftly, she slipped the sticky tape pieces into envelopes and tucked them into her bag. Seconds later, she descended the steps of bus number forty-seven. The deep drone of an engine drew her attention to the back gates. Another bus was arriving.

From behind, a heavy hand gripped her shoulder firmly. "What are you up to, kid?"

The voice belonged to Mr. Three Chins from the front counter. The noise of the bus had masked his footsteps.

"No time to explain. Sorry." She grabbed the man's wrist, bent her back, and heaved at his arm. Despite his solid build, he somersaulted over her shoulder and landed on his back on the oily concrete floor.

Jesse fled.

30.

Liam pulled the car over to the curb. He massaged his shoulder. He had already stopped wearing the sling. It must still have hurt, but he hadn't complained.

Jesse got in.

As Liam accelerated back into the traffic, the driver behind tooted impatiently. "Let me know if you want any driving lessons," said Jesse.

"This is a long way from the hotel. How did you get over to this side of town?"

"In a bag."

"A what?"

"A canvas bag for dirty linen. I fell down the hotel laundry chute. I was escaping from some guys who wanted to find out what I knew, then stop me from talking to anyone else. Permanently."

"OK. Now you have my full attention. Who were these guys?"

"Never seen them before."

He sighed.

"Well, you can't see much when your head's wrapped in sheets."

"Guess not. Start from the beginning. I may not be a genius like you, but if you speak slowly, I should understand."

"I hid in a storage room to listen to the cleaners talking. Then I heard footsteps. This man said they were looking for a kid with crutches. So I jumped down the laundry chute, and that's how I ended up in the bag, then in the van. When the driver stopped, I escaped and messaged you." Jesse turned her head to look out the side window. There was a lot she had omitted — and it was staying that way. If Liam knew about her search for Rohan, she could be in danger. So could Rohan.

"So you were followed to the hotel?"

She shrugged. "I don't think so. I checked

carefully. That man said their contact told them I was there."

As the car slowed, Jesse stared into the windows of a café. It was packed with people — dressed brightly, laughing loudly — normal people who didn't have to worry about who might be behind them.

She dragged her thoughts back to business. "One of those women at the hotel might have recognized Ari's photograph and pretended she didn't. Also, Kingston Martin is staying there under the name Sam Smith. In the king suite."

"Is he now? Interesting connections. Ari and Josef contacted Peace First. Peace First is organizing a rally for tomorrow, where Kingston Martin is a guest speaker. A call was made from the Peace First office to the hotel where Martin is staying. You did well, Jesse."

"The man in the laundry said they had something planned for the rally tomorrow, that nothing must interfere. Do you think Josef wants to kill Kingston Martin at the rally?"

"A logical conclusion."

"But why pick such a public place?"

"Maybe he wants publicity. There would be thousands of eyewitnesses, major media attention. There could be lots of reasons. There are agents watching the Peace First office and Brian Marinelli and Frederica Gordon. Tonight I'll keep watch on the hotel. You don't need to be there. I'll take you back to C2. Get some rest for tomorrow."

"If Ari is in this with Josef, he's not just a janitor, is he?"

"You eaten yet?" asked Liam. "An army marches on its stomach, according to Emperor Napoleon. He took his chef on military campaigns. While Napoleon was fighting, the chef would be back at camp, whipping up a tasty new dish. That's how we got Chicken Marengo. From the Battle of Marengo."

He's avoiding my question. What's he hiding?

ƎI.

Back at C2, Jesse stared at the open doorway of her room, waiting for Jai. She checked her clock. Although the numbers ran counterclockwise, the hands were in the correct place. It was the best gift Prov had given her. Unless something was wrong, Jai would be there in exactly two minutes.

She heard his footsteps in the corridor. Then he appeared in the doorway. As he did every day, he raised his violin to one shoulder, closed his eyes, and played.

Jesse's mind churned with uncomfortable thoughts. She had to tell Jai about her discovery. It wasn't right to keep it from him. Rohan was his concern, too. This was something that must be open and honest between them.

Jai stopped playing and opened his eyes. His gaze lingered on her face. "My composition was too sad?"

She shook her head. "It was beautiful. As always." If she closed her eyes she could imagine Jai as a little old man. He spoke in full sentences, no abbreviations, and with enough long words to make his language seem too sophisticated for his skinny boy's body.

"Then you are feeling sad?" He followed the footprints to the table and gently placed his violin on it.

He made a circle in the air with one hand. She knew he was asking if she had checked the room for listening devices. She nodded and rose to shut the door. Again, she locked it and dragged a chair over to block the handle.

"I have something to show you." She sat at her computer desk with Jai beside her.

Quickly, she found the Branwood School Web site and the intriguing photograph.

Jai sat with his eyes glued to the screen. A nerve twitched under his eye. He touched the screen and whispered, "Rohan."

"I saw him yesterday, Jai. He was in a bus at the museum. I was standing really close as they drove past."

Jai continued to stare. "You *saw* him?"

"Well, I *thought* I did."

Then Jai turned to look at Jesse. "What do you mean?"

"He didn't notice me standing on the sidewalk. I wanted to find out about him before I told you. So today I called the school. I talked to him."

Jai smiled. "What did he say?"

"He stuttered. I thought he was pretending to be someone else. He didn't seem to know me."

"He could not speak freely?"

"He was in a school office, not a prison. And he could have given some sign that he knew who I was. He just hung up on me."

"Perhaps something has happened to him. He may not remember who he is."

"I thought of that, too."

Jai followed the same mental path that she had — and jumped to the same wrong conclusion.

"Close your eyes."

Obediently Jai did so, and clasped both hands over his eyes.

Behind his back, Jesse raided her secret hiding place that she told absolutely no one — not even Jai — about. She brought two sheets of paper back to the desk. "Look at this."

Jai inspected the pages. "How did you get these fingerprints?"

"Pencil lead, brushed on with a feather. I transferred the prints to transparent tape, then onto the page. I lifted them from the bus. I saw the boy grab the metal bar on the seat in front of him."

Jai nodded calmly. "There would be many prints on a bus."

"True. But these were the most recent, an almost perfect set. The bus was in the depot waiting for service. No one has been on it since yesterday. It's a charter bus, not used every day." She pointed to page two. "I got these prints from the exercise bike that used to be Rohan's. There were three sets on it. His, Mary's, and mine."

Jai compared the boy's fingerprints from the bus and those from the exercise bike. "These fingerprints are alike."

"Yes. But not exactly the same. And where is the scar on this set I took from the bus? It's not there."

He shook his head and looked again at the computer screen. "That is someone who more than resembles Rohan. It is identical."

"Jai . . . that isn't Rohan in the photo. It wasn't him on the bus or talking to me on the phone. I think Rohan has a twin. They would have the same DNA, but *not* the same tongue or fingerprints."

The twitch under Jai's eye became stronger. "This other boy . . ."

"Peter."

"Is Peter also a genius?"

"He's interested in computers and science, just like Rohan. But he's at an ordinary school. Nothing special. And there's a sample of his science project posted on this Web site. It's pretty good, but there are gaps in his logic. He left out things that Rohan knew when he was four. Rohan would not have made mistakes like that."

"How could one twin be a genius and not the other?" asked Jai.

"I don't know." Jesse clenched her hands into tight balls. "But the answer to that is important. For all three of us."

32.

The next morning, Jesse mingled with the crowd at the start of the peace rally. Banners and signs rested on protesters' shoulders: *BRAINS NOT BOMBS . . . IF WAR IS THE ANSWER, WE'RE ASKING THE WRONG QUESTION. . . .* A girl on Rollerblades skated past, holding a sign nailed to a wooden stick that read NO HITTING.

Chatter bubbled up as protesters met friends. A man with dreadlocks sticking out from under a rainbow beanie beat a drum. Police officers stood on street corners, ready to stop traffic.

Jesse knew that if anyone from Peace First approached her, he or she would have to look carefully to recognize her. She was dressed in a first aid attendant's uniform. Her shoes had built-up soles. Makeup covered the scratch on her face. Green contact lenses, a black wig, and sunglasses completed her disguise. She carried a small case with a red cross on the side.

Ari and Josef were here. Her instinct was strong and she was learning to listen to it. If Ari was involved in this plan to kill Martin, then she didn't feel so bad about bringing him in to C2.

Suddenly the crowd surged. It was time for the march to begin. Jesse walked with them, weaving in and out, backward and forward. Not so fast that she seemed out of place, but quick enough to see as many protest marchers as possible. It was logical, anyway, that a first aid attendant would do that.

She felt vulnerable without Liam. He had started farther to the front. *"Work your way forward. I'll work back and we'll meet in the middle,"* he'd said.

Jesse wasn't sure whether her stomach was in knots over what might happen during the march or simply because of the strength of the crowd. She had never been in the middle of so many people. It made her feel closed in. If Jai were here, he would probably insist that everyone march in straight lines. This ramshackle drifting would be too much for his orderly mind.

As she moved forward through the crowd, she spotted the Peace First staff, marching behind a massive banner. It was held aloft by Roger and a middle-aged man Jesse recognized from the office. Fred, her grin as wide as a slice of watermelon, was in a wheelchair being pushed by Harmony. The placard attached to the back of her chair read I ROLLED FOR PEACE.

Other marchers recognized Fred. They patted her arm, spoke a few words, called greetings. Children asked for autographs. A little girl tried to hand Fred a helium-filled balloon, but it escaped toward the clouds. *She's important to them.* Jesse wished Director Granger could see this. He thought Fred was just a batty old woman. She was much more than that. But maybe he wouldn't understand. Seeing was not understanding.

Jesse moved on. Ari was the priority. She

had to keep looking for him. If Granger was right, Ari planned to leave the country tonight. Time was running out.

A tall man had dressed as the grim reaper. His flowing black cloak and white skull mask looked sinister. Jesse looked at him more closely. But she didn't think it was either Ari or Josef. His body was too chunky. The other two men were slender.

A clown strode past. Fake red lips stood out against his painted white face. His green curly wig was tilted sideways, revealing tufts of dark hair.

Like a pin drawn to a magnet, Jesse's eyes swung back to the clown. Instead of looking away, he held her glance. Despite the makeup, Jesse could see a scar above his left eye. The lid drooped a little. Ari looked exactly like his photograph.

33.

Immediately Jesse looked away, pretending to lose interest. But she watched the clown from the corner of her eye.

She stooped, pretending to retie her shoe-lace. The crowd surged on either side of her like a tide skirting a rock in the ocean. Jesse messaged Liam immediately on her wrist communicator.

A finger prodded Jesse in the back. "Excuse me."

Startled, she stood and half-turned.

A woman with purple hair said, "Do you have a bandage in there? I've got a blister." She lifted one bare foot to show Jesse.

Washing those feet wouldn't hurt, either.

Jesse opened her case and took out a bandage.

"Don't I have to sign for this?" asked the woman.

Jesse shook her head.

"But last time I signed. They wouldn't give me anything unless I did."

Jesse sidled away. She couldn't be distracted. This was too important.

Where was the clown? She couldn't see him. *I only looked away for a few seconds.* On tiptoe, she stretched to see farther ahead. *A green wig. There he is!* He seemed taller than he had a moment ago. She checked left and right. *Another clown.*

Jesse twisted to see behind her.

A long banner flapping in the wind read CLOWNING AROUND FOR PEACE. Behind it, fifty clowns skipped, made faces at the children, and waved toys. Which one was Ari?

34.

Jesse's heart pounded. Beads of perspiration tickled her top lip.

She saw Liam approaching. His uniform and briefcase matched hers. He had an ear-piece inserted in his right ear. That meant he could communicate with other agents posted along the march route. *Why haven't I got one?* Perhaps the others didn't know who she was. They might wonder why a child was involved. C2 was full of secrets. *I must be a secret, too. The kid who doesn't exist.*

Liam fell into step beside her. "Where is he?"

She shrugged. "He's dressed as a clown."

Liam groaned as he noticed the large

number of clowns. "As if this isn't hard enough . . ."

"Something's not right," she said.

"What do you mean?"

Jesse thought back to when she was a toddler. Mary Holt showed her pictures and asked, "Which of these objects doesn't fit with the others?" *That's it. Something doesn't fit. But what?* She remembered Ari's face in the clown makeup — his ludicrous painted lips, his fake white skin, his eyes.

Suddenly she knew.

Ari had made deliberate and prolonged eye contact. *If you're in disguise, trying to avoid detection, you don't meet your hunter's eyes. You keep a low profile.* It was as though he'd shouted, "Here I am. Come and get me." If he was on an illegal — probably violent — mission, why play silly games that might get him caught? It didn't make sense. And that would mean he knew she was from C2.

Her feet kept her moving with the crowd, even while her mind was occupied. The protesters shouted in unison, "What do we want? *Peace*. When do we want it? *Now*."

"Jesse." Liam's voice broke into her tangled thoughts. "There's something I want you to do."

Uh-oh. Now what?

"I guess you have your doubts about all of this. But I want you to trust me. Even if it's just for today."

His face showed an earnest expression. *So? He's a secret agent. He's used to pretending.*

"Things may not turn out the way you expect. But see it through to the end." Liam checked his wrist communicator. "Kingston Martin has arrived. He's down near the front with his group of hangers-on or bodyguards or whatever he calls them." He ran one hand through his hair. His hair sprung back up immediately, looking just as crazy as before. "We're almost out of time. Let's split up. It's quicker. We have to track that clown. I'll go ahead. You hang back."

Again, Jesse sneaked a look at his face. Perspiration shone on his skin. The lines of his body were tense, nervous. *Is he afraid we're not going to catch Ari — or afraid that we will?*

35.

Liam vanished into the crowd. The noise level had risen. People were excited. How far did the line of protesters go? The woman just in front of Jesse strode along like a racehorse in training. She pushed a three-wheeled stroller. Her child gurgled with pleasure at the fun of whizzing along so fast.

Jesse quickened her steps and caught up to the next line of marchers. She couldn't see Ari. The clowns were nowhere in sight. As Jesse drew level with the young mother pushing the stroller, something caught her eye. Jammed in the back pocket of the stroller was a newspaper. Because it was folded, she couldn't see the entire article, but the head-lines said something about Kingston Martin.

"Excuse me," she said to the young mother, "may I look at your newspaper?"

The young woman handed it over right away. "Keep it. I'm finished with it."

Jesse snapped the newspaper open in a desperate hurry. On the front was a large, clear photograph of Martin and his entourage. Standing next to him, glowering like a dog with distemper, stood a man who Jesse recognized.

She had an instant recollection of lying, breathless, in the big laundry bag. The musty odor, the suffocating sheets around the head, the film of perspiration on her skin — it was all so vivid. And so was her memory of the man with the bald head and beaklike nose.

She stumbled over a bump in the street and closed the newspaper. Kingston Martin's head of security had ordered his men to capture her at the hotel, so that they could squeeze information out of her, then shut her up for good. What sort of behavior was that for someone working for a peace activist?

Troubling thoughts wriggled through her mind. She replayed fragments of old conversations. "Everything must go smoothly tomorrow. . . . We have a cause. . . ." The security guy had called Jesse "the kid." There was something about the way he'd said, "She's history." Then, she'd thought that he was talking about her. But what if he wasn't? What if he meant someone else? Someone linked to their cause?

What had Harmony told her? "Fred's a real hero. . . . People from all over the world ask about her. . . . It'll mean so much to everyone if she speaks at the protest rally."

What if Ari and Josef were *not* going to kill Martin? What if they were working *with* him? Who, then, would be their target? Someone female — someone important — someone who was here at the rally. The answer came to her in a flash: *Fred*.

36.

In the same moment that Jesse suspected Fred was in danger, she spied Ari.

He was walking casually, not far in front. She kept her eyes fixed on him, refusing to be distracted by the commotion around her.

Ari turned his head.

Jesse looked away, pretending to laugh at a child holding a helium-filled balloon.

Ari threw one look over his shoulder, then sidled down an alley.

Jesse followed. She couldn't wait for Liam. She'd lose the target.

She held back at the entrance to the alley, near a family group. The parents were appeasing a crying child who had lost something. A toy, some food, Jesse didn't know what. But the family provided cover.

Ari, vivid in his outlandish clown suit, checked left and right. Then he tugged open a door and vanished into a building.

Anxiously, she sent a message to Liam via her wrist communicator.

If Ari was involved in a plot to hurt Fred, he did not deserve sympathy.

With all her senses alert, Jesse inspected the alley, then nearby windows. It seemed derelict but quiet. Nothing unusual. But she knew there was danger lurking there. At least one killer, probably more.

An amplified voice bounced off the buildings and echoed around the city square. The speeches were about to start. Special invited guests, including Fred, would be assembled on the makeshift stage.

She couldn't wait for Liam. She had to enter that building alone.

Liam's warning from the training session echoed in her mind — *You make the wrong choice, you die.*

37.

It took a few seconds for her eyes to adjust to the darkness of the abandoned building. It was littered with trash. Filthy mattresses and empty food cans lay in one corner.

Something warm and furry ran over Jesse's right foot. She gasped. *A rat. Gross.* She heard tiny scuffling noises, then squeaks.

Treading lightly, trying not to breathe in the sour odor, she crept farther into the building.

Is that footsteps? She listened carefully. *Yes. Someone is heading upstairs.*

Carefully, keeping to the wall side of the stairs, she followed the sound. She stepped over some broken glass, a black shoe, and a ripped T-shirt.

Above her, someone tripped on the stairs, then grunted.

She halted, hardly daring to breathe.

The footsteps kept on climbing.

So did Jesse.

The building was several stories high. She checked behind her. If someone else came from that direction, she'd be in trouble, sandwiched between two enemies.

Voices. Male. Two of them.

The stairs led to the roof. A damaged door hung crookedly on one hinge.

Jesse peered out into the bright sunshine.

Two men, identically dressed in clown suits, stood by a low wall around the edge of the roof area. From up here, they would have a perfect view of the stage in the square where the speakers were to address the rally.

Both men had their backs turned to Jesse. How could she tell them apart? Which one was Ari?

One clown looked impatiently at his watch, then toward the stairway door.

Jesse kept still. She felt as though he was staring right at her. But he couldn't see her standing motionless, blending into the stairwell shadows.

Liam, where are you? Why haven't you returned my message?

A cheer rose from the crowd below. A female voice bellowed peace slogans into the microphone. The crowd chanted the same words. Some of the speaker's words echoed so much they were distorted. But two words traveled clearly — *Frederica Gordon.*

The crowd cheered again.

One of the clowns moved aside. His companion was now fully visible. *That's Ari — on the right. The other man must be Josef.*

Josef held a rifle in his hands. He leaned forward and put his eye to the scope.

38.

A hand clamped over her mouth. Strong arms wrapped around her, holding her firmly.

Jesse struggled, furious that she hadn't heard her attacker approach. She tried to stamp on his feet, but couldn't twist around enough to put much power into it.

Outside on the roof, there was a popping sound.

Below, at ground level, a barrage of screams rose like a mushroom cloud.

No!

"Sssssh," a voice whispered in her ears. Then the arms that held her suddenly let go.

She staggered and spun around, trembling with rage.

Liam held one finger to his lips. He grabbed her arm with one hand and pulled her back against the wall.

She tugged her arm free.

Liam raised his gun and fired.

Ari staggered, clutching his chest with both hands.

Liam shot the wrong man!

Josef, the rifle still in his hands, turned around.

Jesse felt as though she was caught in a nightmare. A clown with a painted smile was aiming a gun at them.

Liam fired again.

Josef dropped his rifle, then collapsed. A red stain spread over the right arm of his clown suit.

Liam dashed over to him and kicked the rifle from his reach. A second kick sent it flying down the filthy stairs.

Ari had somehow managed to clamber to his feet. He was heading for the opposite side of the building, trying to get away.

Jesse took off after him. *How can he run so fast with a wound in his chest?*

He reached the back of the roof area and swayed, dangerously close to the edge. Quietly, almost gracefully, he pitched head-first over the low wall and disappeared.

39.

Before Jesse could do more than gasp, she heard a dull clunk, then a groan from behind. She turned, her heart pounding.

Josef was back on his feet, one sleeve stained red, holding a lump of wood in both hands. Liam crumpled into an untidy heap.

No! Liam! Two shots and he messed up both of them. Does he need glasses?

Josef looked up. Jesse didn't move. She knew he was assessing how much of a threat she was. She could almost hear his brain ticking.

Liam stirred.

Josef raised the lump of wood, ready to strike again. Jesse couldn't leave Liam to have his face rearranged by a maniac. Although he deserved it. If he had arrived a few minutes earlier, Fred would still be alive.

"Excuse me, sir," she called.

Surprised, Josef hesitated.

Steadily, she walked toward him. "Have we met before?"

He leaned his head to one side as if he couldn't quite believe what he was hearing.

"You look familiar. Actually, you look like that movie star. What's his name?" She approached even closer. Without looking at Liam directly, she saw he was moving. "I know. It's that hairy actor with the attitude problem . . . King Kong."

Liam grabbed Josef's ankle.

Josef lost his balance and fell back. He kicked out at Liam. Liam winced.

Ouch. That must've hurt.

All three of them looked up as the loud whirr of rotor blades revealed the approach of a black helicopter. Friend or foe, Jesse had no idea.

Liam and Josef were in a tangle of arms and legs. One went down, then the other. Jesse couldn't find an opening to strike. Arms and fists flew in and out as though there was a mob of men fighting instead of just two. There was a sickening crunch as Josef's fist met Liam's nose. Blood spurted across his face.

That's not going to improve your looks. Come on, Liam. Add weight. Hit with your whole body behind the punch.

Liam scrambled to his feet, hands up in a martial arts pose. Josef did the same.

The helicopter closed in. Jesse knew that they had to get out of there. Quickly. One mangled clown was lying in a grotty side street and another was trying to punch Liam's head in. That didn't do a lot for the reputation of clowns.

Wind from the rotor blades blew strands of Jesse's wig hair across her face. Impatiently, she brushed it aside. *That helicopter's getting too close. This fight has to stop now. She thought of Fred in her Hillview dining room. Is there something I can throw?* A quick check told her no. There was a lot of trash strewn about, but nothing round or hard enough to hurl.

Jesse dashed to a small heap of worn car

tires, grabbed the nearest one, and headed for the two men. She climbed onto the edge of a raised skylight behind them. Briefly, she caught Liam's eye, and held the tire aloft.

He gave a tiny nod, just before Josef's leg connected with his stomach. Liam bent double, groaning loudly. He lashed out and shoved Josef with both hands.

Josef staggered back, closer to Jesse. She leaped from the skylight, high into the air, holding the tire out in front of her. Neatly, it slipped over Josef's head and jammed on his shoulders. He tipped over, sideways. With no hands free to break his fall, his head cracked on the cement. Josef's eyes rolled back. His legs twitched, but he made no move to get up.

Jesse stared at him.

Holding a handkerchief to his nose, Liam knelt beside Josef and touched his fingers under Josef's jaw. "Strong pulse, thumb sucker. He's just unconscious."

Just? Jesse's legs shook, threatening to let her down. *I did that.*

The helicopter hovered closer, then landed on the clearest part of the rooftop. Grit blew into Jesse's face. She coughed and spat from her lips.

"Do we have to run again?" she asked, eyeing the helicopter.

Liam grabbed her arm. "Get in the chopper."

40.

In the helicopter, Jesse sat wedged between the pilot and Liam. The rotor blades were so noisy that she, Liam, and the pilot had to wear earphones.

Liam's nose had stopped bleeding, but there were still crimson smears across his cheeks.

The bird's-eye view of the city would normally have fascinated her. Yet today, she couldn't get excited about it. *Poor Fred.* Jesse felt as though she had indigestion. Pain clutched at her chest and stomach.

What would Granger do when he found out that Liam had shot Ari? She and Liam were partners. They would both be blamed. And punished.

Exactly twenty minutes after they boarded the helicopter, they entered Granger's waiting room, three floors below ground level.

Providenza, the officer manager, looked up as the outer door slid open. Her eyes, heavy with mascara and eyeliner, popped wide open. Her teased hair dwarfed her face. Prov sent Jesse a sympathetic look, but said nothing. Jesse bet she didn't know *what* to say. Neither did Jesse.

Liam and Jesse still wore their first aid uniforms, but Jesse had removed her wig. It felt tight, like hands gripping her skull.

"It'll be all right," whispered Liam.

Oh really? Jesse raised one eyebrow.

Behind the closed doors of the inner office, voices rumbled in conversation.

Suddenly, the inner door was flung open. Granger stood there. "Come in, you two."

Jesse's legs shook so much that she had to concentrate to walk properly. They threatened to give way altogether when she saw Director Granger's visitor.

41.

Ari stood in Granger's office. Smiling, healthy, and uninjured. He leaned forward to shake hands with Liam.

Jesse shot a look at her partner's face. He didn't look surprised.

No longer the clown, Ari wore a pair of brown trousers and an open-necked shirt. Most of his face paint had been wiped off, but one or two streaks remained in his hair. His hair was now dark and short instead of green and fluffy. A bandage was wrapped around one ankle.

Ari held his hand out to Jesse. She couldn't remember offering her own, but she must have, because suddenly he was shaking it.

His palm was warm and dry. Ari's gaze was piercing, as though he were examining her brain as well as her face. Uncomfortable, she withdrew her hand and stepped back.

Granger smiled.

He's going to order our executions. He never smiles.

"Liam and Jesse," said Granger. "Sit down. I thought you might like to meet our newest addition to C2. As you know, this is Ari."

"Why aren't you dead?" asked Jesse, tired of all the twisted games C2 made them play.

"Our *dear* Jesse likes to come directly to the point," said Granger. He emphasized *dear* as though it were a swear word.

Ari sat down beside Jesse. "My injury was staged. I was not shot. When Liam fired the gun into the air, I clutched my chest, breaking a capsule of red dye. There was a truck waiting in the alley below. I landed in soft material that was piled in the back. I knocked the wind out of myself and twisted this ankle. But that is nothing."

Nothing? He fell several floors onto the back of a truck and it's nothing?

"I am defecting to this country . . . to this

organization. I could not cooperate any more with the things my own country asked me to do."

Jesse kept a straight face, but her mind twisted and turned. *I know how you feel.*

"If I tried to leave, the authorities would punish my family. I could not smuggle them all out and I could not leave them in danger. So I had to die."

Liam grunted.

"They will not hunt for a dead man. Now I am a hero. I died doing my duty. My family will be looked after."

"But won't your family be upset?" asked Jesse.

Ari's jaw worked for a moment before he spoke. "Yes, but they will be safe. And one day, I will return to take them away."

I hope they'll still remember you.

She wondered when Ari would realize that he had run into an organization that was much like the country he had just fled.

"Do you have any more questions you wish to ask me?" said Ari.

"No," said Liam.

"Yes," said Jesse. "Did you shoot at us in the cemetery?"

He gave a pathetic smile. "It was Josef. We were watching the Peace First office when Josef recognized Liam. He planted a tracker on the vehicle and followed you to the old woman. Josef worried you might be working out the connections."

Liam growled. "That car was clean."

"We have new technology that your old scanners do not detect."

Granger leaned forward. "I would be interested in the details of that."

Ari inclined his head. "I am here to help."

Suspicious, Jesse watched his face carefully. What was his real purpose in being here?

42.

Following their meeting in Director Granger's office, Liam directed Jesse to the briefing room and closed the door. Liam sat gingerly. His face was swollen, his eyelids heavy. There was the promise of a black eye.

"You knew about that setup," she said.

He looked away. "Only since yesterday. I was ordered to keep quiet. The fewer people who knew, the less chance of leaks."

Jesse's thoughts swung back to Fred.

Liam's wrist communicator vibrated. He checked the message and smiled. "You were right. Frederica Gordon was selected as a target. But not by Josef. By Kingston Martin."

"Martin! But he's a peace activist."

"He fought for peace. That's the same as dieting to be fat. He had certain goals in mind and didn't care how he accomplished them."

He should've applied for a job with C2.

"Martin wanted a martyr, someone who would die for a cause. He chose Fred. A dead leader can have more power than a live one. She couldn't make mistakes. Followers would remember only the best things she did, the wisest of her sayings. They'd give her attributes she didn't have. She may have had more power to rally people in death than in her life. Kingston could use the protesters' anger to bring about change. He probably figured one sacrifice was worth the result."

Jesse rested her chin on her clasped hands. "But he broke his principles by having her murdered."

"Actually, she's alive and probably already planning who to throw oranges at next."

Jesse sat bolt upright.

"Before Kingston and his men could carry out their vicious plan, Josef took him out."

"Who is Josef, really?"

"An agent for a foreign government. Ari was sent along as a test of his loyalty."

Some test.

"The message I just received said that Josef has escaped. When the other agents got to the rooftop, he was no longer there. All they found was a clown suit and a bunch of old tires."

"He was meant to escape, wasn't he?"

Liam nodded. "Now he can go home and tell the story of his companion, who died in the line of duty."

"But you shot Josef."

He smiled. "Fine marksmanship, even if I do say so myself. I shot to wound. Tricky business. It was necessary to bring in Ari safely. If Josef had become suspicious, he would have removed Ari instantly. I admit our assignment was more difficult than I anticipated. Josef is clever. We couldn't find them. You have to admire talent like that. He stuck to Ari like superglue. Ari couldn't get a message to us to say where he was."

Jesse looked at Liam across the table. His face was swelling by the minute. He looked distorted, as though his features were squeezed Play-Doh.

In that moment, a truth became clear to her. Liam allowed Josef to shoot Martin so that Fred would be safe. Director Granger would not have ordered him to do that. Granger didn't care what happened to Fred. Jesse was also sure Liam would never admit it.

43.

That night, right after her time with Jai, Jesse headed for the gym. Although she was tired, so much was whizzing through her mind that she knew she would not sleep. Perhaps exercise would relax her.

She stayed on the treadmill for an hour, till her legs went past the rubbery stage into numbness.

Gradually, she slowed the machine.

Behind her, someone came into the room. She looked over her shoulder.

"Good evening," said Ari. "I'm just taking a look around, becoming accustomed to where things are situated."

Dubious about his true reason for being in the gym, she stepped from the treadmill.

Ari limped between the pieces of equipment, touching each lightly with his fingers. *So his twisted ankle was for real.* The scar beside his left eye stood out.

Jesse wondered how he felt, being alone here. No family, no friends. Yet *his* family was alive.

"You are wondering about my scar," said Ari.

She shrugged.

"I was beaten in prison. I would not obey the authorities. I was wondering about *your* scars."

"I don't have any."

"Not all scars are on the outside."

Jesse didn't answer. She didn't want to get involved in a conversation with this man. He made her uncomfortable. Before he could frame another awkward question that she could not answer, she fired one at him. "Why did Josef kill Kingston Martin?"

"Martin murdered our leader's nephew. At first, our government knew who Kingston was and did nothing. His activities suited them. But then it became personal."

Jesse picked up her towel and mopped perspiration from her face.

"In case you are wondering, I am not a killer. My skills are in other areas," said Ari. "I was forced to accompany Josef to test my loyalty and commitment. It has been his task for many years to keep watch over me. He was good at his work."

Why did Ari's government go to all that trouble to keep an eye on him? And why would C2 go through all this elaborate plotting to bring him in? Some secret about Ari made him valuable.

She raised an eyebrow. "You're not really a janitor, are you?"

He sat on a bench seat and poked at a set of hand weights, with no intention of picking them up. "Indeed I was. Part of my punishment for disobedience. Menial work in the laboratory I used to run."

Laboratory? Despite the heat her exercise had generated, Jesse shivered.

"I am a medical scientist," said Ari.

I've helped bring in a man who's going to work in the laboratory. Her past experiences in the C2 laboratory gave her an overwhelming longing to get as far away from him as possible. She threw the towel over her shoulder and headed toward the door.

She had been right at the beginning, when she had suspected that Ari's identity was a cover. But she had not predicted this. No wonder Director Granger hadn't explained the true facts.

Jesse looked back, just once, and met Ari's eyes. It wasn't a casual look. He was interested in her. He knew about her. The Director had brought Ari here for Operation IQ, she'd bet on it. What, exactly, were they planning? One thought flashed in her mind like a neon light — *I've rescued my enemy.*

Here's a sneak peek at

UNDERCOVER GiRl
#3...nightmare

1.

The face was monstrous, distorted. Eyes wider than normal, square snout, and a long jaw.

Jesse stared. *Creepy.*

It was late, and dark. Street lights cast a pathetic, eerie glow. She couldn't read his facial expressions. But that was not unusual. Like her, he was good at hiding things. Even when his face wasn't behind a mask.

"We could start a new fashion trend," whispered Liam, his voice muffled.

"If you want to look like a mutant pig." Jesse hoped her own masked face didn't look as weird as Liam's. Although, with his pale, pockmarked skin, crooked nose, and tousled hair, Liam would never make a list of the most beautiful people.

Still in a crouching position, Liam pressed the tiny light button on his watch, then released it. "Forty-five seconds to go."

Jesse nodded. Her heart beat faster. *What if someone catches us?* She gave a tiny shrug. In a way, she was already a prisoner. The secret organization C2 made sure of that. The word *prisoner* had not occurred to her before. But it was true. Her mind flashed a dictionary definition, *a person or thing confined by another's grasp.* She often wished her extraordinary memory would disappear. It recalled things she wanted to forget.

"Gas will be circulating through the air-conditioning system by now. The guards will be falling unconscious. Don't remove your mask till we're out and away." Liam's breathing, inside his own gas mask, sounded strange, exaggerated.

It's like being on a stakeout with Darth Vader, thought Jesse.

"Ready?" he asked.

She patted the tiny flash drive that hung on a chain around her neck. Only the size and weight of a pack of chewing gum, it had plenty of space for the files she had to download from the computer. The building floor plan was imprinted in her memory. Yet, hot prickles swept the back of her neck. Her instincts were sending her a warning. Even from out here, she didn't like this place. Didn't want to go inside.

"I know what I have to do," she said. "I just don't know *why*."

Liam turned, aiming the chunky nose of his gas mask in her direction once again. "You don't need to know why. Just do it. Jesse Sharpe, you ask too many questions."

"I'm a kid. Kids ask questions."

He shook his head. "No. You're a C2 agent. None of us are anything else but agents. We can't be if we want to stay alive. Remember that. Wait ten seconds, then follow." He shot forward, immediately absorbed into the darkness.

Jesse tensed, ready to run.

Nervously, she looked up at the illuminated *Cryohome* sign on the roof of their targeted building. They were about to break into a place that froze dead people.